GOLDEN DRAGON

Also by V.E. Ulett

The Blackwell's Adventures series

Captain Blackwell's Prize

Blackwell's Paradise

Blackwell's Homecoming

GOLDEN DRAGON
V. E. ULETT

CHAPTER ONE

On a bright August morning Miriam Kodio Blackwell made a slow and seemingly purposeless circuit to the end of the quay facing the Bay of Algiers. Men trundled barrels of wine and oil to the waiting ships, and stacked bales of tobacco secured with fibre cord near the ships' gangways. Bleating goats and poultry squawking in their cages protested the fate of becoming ship's stores. Miriam carefully avoided the most crowded areas of loading and unloading, wearing a *burqa* that concealed her from head to ankles. Moving with a stooped and old gait, Miriam's youthful mind focused on the Dey of Algiers' fleet at anchor in port, and on a knot of Englishmen near a boat at the end of the quay.

She carried a market basket heavy with figs, dates, citrus fruits, jars of oysters cured in spiced oil, and other sundries. Miriam set it down on the wooden walkway while she gazed at the Algerian navy, all in port. Four 44-gun frigates, five large corvettes of 24 to 30 guns apiece, and several score of gun and mortar boats. From the age of ten, when she was evacuated out of Ceuta in a British Royal Navy ship, Miriam felt an especial connection to ships and she'd made a study of them. James Blackwell, the captain of that British warship was the brother of Miriam's step-father, the diplomat Francis Blackwell. Through Francis, Miriam retained connections to both the British navy and foreign service.

It was the British foreign service Miriam turned to when Iran became too hot for her. The young English captain Miriam observed now pacing beside his gig, tied up to the quay under a flag of truce, was in an uncomfortable position as well. He was surrounded by the enemy, and awaiting the Dey's pleasure. Since it was the head of a clandestine branch of the British diplomatic service that arranged Miriam's passage from Iran to France and then Algiers, she knew of the confrontation looming between the Dey of Algiers and the British.

She was there to play her part in the conflict, and with a halting shuffle Miriam moved toward the handsome English captain. He was the unfortunate messenger sent to carry the British list of demands to the Dey, ruler of the fortified City of Algiers. The Dey was holding nineteen British hostages. An entire boat's crew, including a surgeon and two midshipmen, had been stopped, seized, and were being kept under guard. The British consul and his family were also sequestered, at the consul's residence in Algiers. Miriam stepped into the path the English captain was wearing in the planks of the quay.

Arriving in his circuit back at his gig, the English captain trod on the hem of Miriam's long robe. Arrested in mid-stride they both staggered, Miriam's market basket flying from her grasp.

"I beg your pardon, madam."

The captain reached out and gripped Miriam by the upper arm to steady her. A surprised expression came over his face as his long elegant fingers closed on her rounded flesh, not the flab and bone of an old woman he'd been expecting. He peered at Miriam, ducking his head as he tried to examine her through the covering of her *burqa*.

"St. George or St. Denis?" he said, gently releasing Miriam's arm.

"St. George, in course," she replied.

The captain gave a nod to his coxswain, who discreetly lifted a woven basket from the gig to the planks of the quay.

"What say you to Code Black?" The captain's voice was full of authority.

"Kodio Blackwell at your service, sir."

His rigid posture and stern stare relaxed at once. The captain's tone became familiar, as though they'd just been presented at a country ball. "May I say, your English is perfect. I thought it all great mummery, this part of the mission, when his lordship—" The captain coughed, recollecting himself. "My name is Dashwood, ma'am, Captain Dashwood of HMS *Prometheus*. It is my boat's crew the Dey has thrown in his dungeon. I was told to offer any assistance possible to you, ma'am."

"The family names of the Dey's ministers, then, if you please. And directions to the residence of the British consul."

As Dashwood spoke, pronouncing the foreign names with difficulty, Miriam bent over the baskets. She appeared not to be attending to him, meanwhile shifting a length of cotton cloth from her basket to cover the contents of the one he'd brought.

She straightened, but not to her full height, and stood before him in a bent posture, his basket on her arm.

"How long have you been waiting, if I may be so bold, Captain Dashwood?"

"Two hours, or very near."

She was silent a moment, and then lifted her chin slightly and allowed Dashwood's soft eyes to met her gaze. "Return to your ship, *Raiz*," she said. "It's the most prudent course. You have been made to wait long enough, it is an insult in the Arab world. Send to the Dey that you shall return tomorrow for his response, when you must also collect the young gentlemen taken from your command."

He stared at her, trying to catch her eye again.

"Peace be with you, infidel."

She hobbled slowly away after uttering this phrase in Arabic, and melted into the crowd of bearers on the quay. A refined gentleman like Captain Dashwood would appreciate the basket of delicate edibles she'd left him, and possibly even the two bottles of scented rose water.

It cost Miriam a great deal of maneuvering to be admitted to the presence of the British consul, and when she was at last led in to Lord Elgin she thought the joy on his face at sight of her would give the game away. The captain of the guards implanted on the British, Shakeel Ahmed Ansari, was a sharp-eyed, hawk nosed creature. She'd presented herself to him as Miriam Albuyeh, sent by Saud Kodio, minister and first cousin to the Dey of Algiers. Captain Ansari was an old experienced soldier, unmoved by beautiful dark eyes or a well shaped ankle, and as keen as his raptor features. Miriam didn't exactly trade on the name of Kodio; she was the daughter of the former Dey of Oran, Ali Khosrow ibn Kodio, whose throat was cut by his brother; she merely impressed upon Ansari both the Kodio's punctilio and their inclination toward vengeance. Fortunately, Lord Elgin recovered before Captain Ansari noticed anything amiss.

"I thought you were to bring a wet nurse, Captain," Lord Elgin cried. "This maid is barely out of leading strings."

"Calm yourself. It is not easy to find one in a city that is being evacuated of women and children," Ansari said. "Allow me to present Miss Miriam Albuyeh, sent by the Dey's ministers to safeguard the honor of your lady wife and daughter. Since your own servants have seen fit to accept the Dey's generous invitation to quit your employ."

A baby's loud wailing started up in another part of the house, and both men cringed.

"Perhaps you would be so good, Captain," Miriam said, "as to send for ass's or goat's milk. Whichever may be easier to come by, while I become acquainted with the household?"

Shakeel Ahmed Ansari bowed, eager to take his leave.

"Merry Blackwell!" Lord Elgin said, once they were alone. "How glad I am to see you."

"How do you do, Lord Elgin," Miriam said, unsure how she felt about anyone besides her step-father Francis using that name. It was his ironic little joke, since Miriam had never been exactly merry. "And how are Lady Elgin and Fanny? I do not need to ask how your dear son does, the poor baby."

"I shall take you to them directly, and to meet little Tommy. But first please do be seated. I would offer you refreshment, but we are utterly at the mercy of our heathen hosts for viands. What a welcome sight you are, Miss Blackwell, for I make sure you were sent by Lord Q."

"Oh yes," Miriam said, "of course I was. Government is demanding an indemnity for the massacre of the Italian fishermen, and the liberation of Christian slaves, along with the immediate release of yourself and all British subjects."

Miriam observed the unhappy purse of Lord Elgin's lips, and inwardly she sighed. "I am sent to escort your wife and daughter out before the bombing of the City commences. Lord Exmouth and the English and Dutch fleets come for you, sir, and Captain Dashwood's men."

A smile lit the diplomat's face, over news that the enemy's actions should have already confirmed to him. Were they not preparing for a siege? She supposed Lord Elgin needed reassurance that his government was sending more than just a woman to his aid.

The pitch of the baby's cry changed to one of desperation. Miriam would have been astonished to see Lord Elgin sitting with hands folded before his child's distress, in an attitude of intense inward concentration, had she not seen the like a hundred times before. She rose. "Allow me to check on that milk, sir."

Miriam didn't find the cook house deserted, though Lord Elgin's personal servants may have fled. She paused before entering and making her presence known, to observe the people. A man whose tight turban rested atop a mountain of cheek and jowl was in charge, and speaking the loudest. "...and His Highness has invited the City to watch the destruction of the heathen ships. The English sailors will be white washing the palace walls by evening prayers!" His audience, a kitchen boy and two *sous* chefs, guffawed.

"Ah, *Hanim*!" the fat cook cried out to Miriam, the moment she set foot in the kitchen. "We have been expecting you. The good Captain Ansari left specific orders. He has gone away, you see, to attend to the disposition of his guns and men. He is given command of a pair of guns of the middle battery guarding the North Mole. A most honored position, Allah be praised."

Miriam inclined her head and made the appropriate noises. The cook wanted her to notice his pride in following Captain Ansari, he was not a common servant or house slave.

"The milk for the babe?" she said.

One of the assistant chefs lifted a spoonful of the milk he stirred in a saucepan over the fire, for Miriam to taste.

Nodding her approval, Miriam said, "But, oh! What to put it in?"

"With respect, *hanim*." The cook stepped forward. "I, Atif Mehmood, am responsible for provisioning and feeding Captain Ansari's regiment. Sometimes a goat's kid will refuse the teat, and a baby goat being a valuable creature, why! in that case I will use this."

He brought from behind his back, with a little flourish, a jar ready filled with the good warm milk. Fastened over the top with much knotted twine was the end of a prophylactic, if Miriam did not mistake.

Miriam stared at Atif Mehmood, her expression placid and neutral. She searched but found no cunning jest, no awkward misplaced lasciviousness in the cook's demeanor. His smile widened when she reached out and took the jar he offered. In her slender hand it looked even more abominable.

"I thank you, Atif Mehmood, and so will the babe. Direct me to the apartment with my dunnage, if you please," Miriam said.

The cook bowed to her, and straightened with a self-satisfied smile.

Back in the cool luxury of the British consul's residence, the first thing that greeted Miriam was the baby's cry. She followed the sound of the wailing to the door of a sitting room, and knocked.

No response came from within, though Miriam heard the rustling of skirts and the baby's uninterrupted howling. She opened the door and stepped over the threshold.

"Miss Blackwell?" Lady Elgin declared, starting up. "We thought it was those filthy heathens, we never willingly admit *them* to our presence. I cannot tell you how happy I am to see a friendly face."

Miriam gazed over at the baby, who lay sprawling and kicking, shrieking himself red, upon the sofa.

"How do you do, Ma'am? How do you do, Fanny? This must be little Tommy."

"My precious boy!" Lady Elgin cried, though she didn't move to comfort him. "How can the Dey be so cruel as to make a little child suffer so? Yet he must have something of humanity, for he has allowed you to come to us in our hour of need."

Miriam went to sit beside the shrieking child, set down the jar of milk, and cast her eye about the room. She discovered her own basket in a corner, and suppressed the urge to go over and make sure the contents had not been disturbed.

"Miss Fanny, is there any such thing as a sewing basket in the room?"

Fanny instantly brought her own work basket, and Miriam extracted a pair of small shears. With a little purse of her lips, Miriam nipped the end of the prophylactic. She gathered up the squalling Tommy, pinned his flailing arms and legs against her body, and pointed the pierced end of the shield into his mouth.

The poor child, yellow and skinny though he was, latched onto the artificial nipple. Tommy sucked fiercely, shaking his head as though tearing meat from the bone. She forced him to take breath every so often by lowering the jar so no milk was flowing. Just when he was set to shriek again, Miriam raised the jar to continue his meal.

"Why do you tease him so?" Lady Elgin demanded. "Let the poor child have all he wishes. Send to those blackguards to prepare more milk."

But on her lowering the milk jar just as Lady Elgin finished her outcry, Tommy's eyes rolled back in ecstasy. His lips continued to move in a sucking motion, and gradually Miriam fed him the last of the milk. Growing up in the Dey of Oran's harem, amid an extended family of half brothers and sisters, someone always had a baby. Miriam was accustomed to their ways.

Tommy's loud belch as Miriam held him up against her shoulder was punctuated by a tap on the door. Lord Elgin ducked his head around the door, and Lady Elgin and Fanny at once jumped to their feet crying out. Only Miriam remained seated with the sleeping baby on her shoulder. Tommy had apparently been both hungry and exhausted.

"You are a godsend, Miss Blackwell," Lord Elgin said, leading his two ladies to seats near her.

He caught sight of the instrument with which Miriam had been succoring his son, and frowned.

"Just what I was saying!" Lady Elgin said. "The Dey has been kind in sending a nurse, and I am not ungrateful believe me, Miss Blackwell. But what about us? How long are we to remain captives?"

Lady Elgin made great cow eyes at Lord Elgin, who glanced at Miriam. Miriam eased Tommy onto the sofa, placing pillows round to close him in.

"I was not sent by the Dey, your ladyship," Miriam said. "Though that is what I told your guards."

She rose and retrieved her basket. Bringing it back to her seat, Miriam quickly reviewed the contents. Underneath a bolt of homespun cloth and the *burqa* she'd been wearing, were Miriam's second gown, and, below a false bottom in the basket, two complete British midshipman's uniforms. Minus the side arms, in course.

"Tomorrow you and I and Miss Fanny will meet *Prometheus's* boat at the quay, and Captain Dashwood will carry you to Gibraltar." Miriam lifted a naval jacket and breeches from the bottom of the basket. "Disguised, wearing these."

Lady Elgin gave a gasp, and Fanny a slight squeal. Both women's gazes flew to Lord Elgin, who sadly nodded.

"Indeed, it must be so," he said. "Even the heathens are evacuating their women. That is why there is to be no wet nurse."

"What of you, Thomas, are you to remain a prisoner? And little Tommy!" Lady Elgin flew to the baby, and mashed his pillows against him. "I will not leave my baby!"

Once again Lord Elgin turned to Miriam.

"Orders are for the women," Miriam said. "You and Miss Fanny, to be brought out."

Much had been left in her own hands, which was what she preferred. Lord Q wanted the British consul, his family, and suite entire got out, if possible. To smuggle out the British consul would be a near impossibility, Miriam felt, and his baby son's presence in the house was some protection and safeguard for the father. That was what the British did not realize.

"Orders! What do I care for orders!"

"Please, Constance, do try to calm down. For the baby's sake." Lord Elgin glanced fearfully at Tommy, lest the fuss wake him.

Tommy frowned in his sleep.

"I will not be moved, and so I warn you." Lady Elgin glared at Lord Elgin and Miriam. "Unless Tommy is to go too." She sat eagerly forward, turning her back on the baby. "We can hide him in a basket. Much like your own, Miss Blackwell, except with a lid."

"He will cry, your ladyship, and give us all away," Miriam said. "What Captain Ansari's men will do if we are discovered, I cannot tell."

Whatever it was the retribution would be worse for her than for her ladyship and Fanny.

"You can give him a sleeping draught," Lady Elgin enthused. "You people are skilled at potions and elixirs, are you not?"

Miriam stared at her, an even, level gaze revealing nothing of her inward feelings. Her hand itched to deal out a slap. Slaps for being an ignorant, insolent sod she'd also seen plenty of in the harem. The scandal and unwanted union she'd fled in Iran, the reasons Miriam became involved with these British aristocrats, were now a distant evil. Whereas the mortification of that phrase *you people*, was very much a present one.

CHAPTER TWO

Dashwood paced the quay once more, trailed by a slight young midshipman from the flagship *Queen Charlotte*. *Prometheus's* own two young gentlemen continued to enjoy the Dey's hospitality. Since their meeting the day before, the little enigma in veiled garb, Miss Kodio Blackwell, was much on Dashwood's mind. He constantly scanned the crowd hoping to catch sight of a dark flashing gaze, from the most enchanting pair of eyes.

Today there was even more activity on the quay, and within the massive batteries along the waterfront. The place was swarming with soldiers and civilians. The great wave of sweating people filing down to the water's edge and milling about the quay surprised and rather horrified Dashwood.

A festival atmosphere prevailed complete with vendors of oranges, dates, and skewered meats. The sellers jostled through the bodies, crying out and waving their fragrant wares overhead. Dashwood gathered the natives were expecting a show, anticipating the British ships would be blown out of the water. For a small city, the fortifications of Algiers were mighty. The batteries protecting the anchorage and waterfront together mounted 220 guns, of 32, 24 and 18 pounder cannons.

The British fleet was lying becalmed at the western end of the Bay of Algiers. Sir Edward Pellew, Admiral Lord Exmouth, was commander in chief of the combined British and Dutch forces. His lordship dispatched Dashwood, Lieutenant Burgess, and two of Queen Charlotte's midshipmen to the Dey for a response to Britain's demands. The Dey's port admiral met *Prometheus's* boat and escorted the chosen officers, Mr. Burgess and Mr. Kirker, into the hostile city.

As time passed and the British delegation did not return, Dashwood began to reconsider. He had no wish to see that young woman—she must be young with her sweet feminine voice and gaze—in the middle of a dangerous action. After pacing the crowded quay for more than an hour, Dashwood was almost relieved when an uproar broke out near the entrance gate. By aggressive use of his elbows, Dashwood opened a lane toward the commotion, with little midshipman Richards in his wake.

Ahead he could just make out two sets of British uniforms. The first two figures in Royal Navy blue were passing the military guard, followed by a crowd of bearers. Among the porters and not far behind two mincing midshipmen, was an elegant woman striding beside a man with a large woven basket balanced on his head. Her hair was covered, but Dashwood strained and caught a glimpse of an oval face and large luminous eyes. Her attention was focused on the man with the basket, and then the man stumbled, nearly upsetting his load.

A child's loud bawling erupted, followed by shouts from the guards. The cry was taken up by soldiers loitering outside their gun embrasures. As Dashwood struggled to make out what had become of the woman and the basket, the first of those two midshipmen reached him and fell upon his breast.

He was forced to turn immediately for *Prometheus's* boat, with the sobbing woman in midshipman's dress under his arm. He signaled to Richards to take the arm of the second midshipman. Miss Fanny Bruce was faring better than her mama, who was wailing incoherently. The common people on the quay edged away from her, as they would before a mad woman.

Dashwood wanted to turn back after handing her into the boat, go up the quay and investigate. Where was Miss

Kodio Blackwell, with what must have been the Consul's infant son in that basket? He was sure it was her face—those eyes!—he'd glimpsed in the crowd. Lieutenant Burgess and Midshipman Kirker came pelting up; they'd been the second set of uniforms he'd spotted in the crowd. Once they leapt in the boat, Dashwood couldn't justify waiting longer.

"Pull away," he ordered. "Steer for the flag, Sims."

Lady Elgin was sobbing on Lieutenant Burgess' gold-laced shoulder. The lieutenant shook his head sadly at Dashwood. Free of that encumbrance, Dashwood craned round and stared back at the quay. A captain of artillery jumped up on the outside of his gun embrasure and shouted down into the crowd. Whatever the man heard in response from the tangled mass of people below made him draw his sword. The Algerian glared directly at Dashwood as the boat pulled away, and shook his sword at him.

The artillery captain then sheathed his weapon, running along the outside of the gun embrasures, and jumping down level by level, until he was on the quay and swallowed up by the crowd. A sick dread and apprehension filled Dashwood for the woman they were leaving behind.

"Oh!" Miriam cried. "Captain Ansari, how glad I am to see you!"

Shakeel Ahmed Ansari pushed his way through the knot of people surrounding Miriam and Tommy, lying squalling and furious in the open basket. Atif Mehmood was beside her; the cook had answered Captain Ansari's hail.

"Fire on them, Captain! The British women, they are making away in that boat! When I could not find them at the Consul's residence, I followed them here."

"The little squaller gave them away," Atif Mehmood added helpfully. "They were dressed in men's uniforms, the sluts!"

Captain Ansari shot a furious scowl at Atif Mehmood, and whirled about to stare at the rapidly retreating boat. Then he glanced down at Tommy, kicking and screaming.

"No, it will not do. They are already out of range, the English dogs, and orders are orders. We are not to fire first."

He turned a penetrating gaze on Miriam. She pursed her lips and leaned over the basket, allowing her head scarf to shield her face.

"I know what you are thinking, Miss," the Captain said. "What kind of benighted creature runs away dressed as a man, and leaves behind her own son? It is an offense to God."

Miriam straightened and met Captain Ansari's fierce stare. "It is an offense you shall avenge." She cast her eyes upward to Captain Ansari's gun emplacement.

His gun's crew had come out from their positions and were gaping at them over the edge of the gun embrasure.

"Lieutenant Saed!" Captain Ansari called. While the nimble lieutenant made his way down to them, Ansari mumbled to Miriam, "The heathen dogs will not cause me to miss the first shots of this battle!" The Captain raised his voice. "Lieutenant Saed, escort Miss Albuyeh and the baby to the Consul's residence. And when you get there, I want him clapped in irons! Do you hear? Shackle him in the small downstairs sitting room, leave one guard, bring the rest and report as fast as ever you can. We shall need every man."

Captain Ansari's keen dark eyes were on the war ships sailing into the Bay of Algiers. Before she left with the lieutenant, Captain Ansari said to Miriam, in a private aside, "It is a good thing you are here to look after the baby, Miss Albuyeh. It is more humanity than the infidels deserve."

Miriam gave him a wide-eyed look. It was never difficult to convince a man she was stupider than she was.

Lieutenant Saed wasn't eager to leave the quay before the first shots were fired, pushing his way through the crowd with so little enthusiasm that they hadn't passed the guard at the gate. Consequently Miriam was there when, a sea breeze coming up, the fleet sailed in and took up stations half a pistol shot from the quay and the breakwater behind which lay the entire Algerian navy. Even Tommy was no longer bawling. One of the sweets sellers had taken pity on him, and given the boy a sugar teat. From Miriam's arms Tommy nodded his infant head round at the scene while he sucked.

The massive three-decker 100-gun *Queen Charlotte* was brought to just at the mouth of the anchorage near the breakwater. Her crew began lashing her to an Algerian brig moored quayside. Three more heavy British frigates of 40 to 50-guns each sailed in and took up stations ahead in line of *Queen Charlotte*, so that the British two and three deckers' starboard guns bore on the Fish Market Battery and the City to the southwest. More heavy British ships were taking up stations aft of *Queen Charlotte*, from the breakwater in a line running northeasterly. The Bay of Algiers was filled with hundreds of sails. Smaller British ships, the sloops and bomb vessels, were sailing behind the line of battle ships.

The crowd on the quay was all agape at the spectacle, including Captain Ansari's artillerymen and many other guns' crews, watching the British fleet from outside their gun embrasures.

"A prodigious fine sight maybe," Lieutenant Saed said. "But are not they taking a precious long time to anchor?"

Miriam shrugged and shook her head. Besides lashing the flag to the Algerian brig, as an aid to the rest of the fleet in taking up their proper positions, *Queen Charlotte* would be mooring with springs to her cables; lines that could be pulled on to swing her tremendous broadside to bear in different directions. When a signal broke out aboard *Queen Charlotte*, Miriam took firmer hold of Tommy and began tunneling through the crowd.

Lieutenant Saed had no choice but to follow. Signal flags were racing up to the yardarms of the nearest British ships. Miriam looked back, and so close were they that she could make out a cluster of officers aboard *Queen Charlotte*. The most resplendently clad figure on *Queen Charlotte's* quarterdeck was gesturing at the soldiers and artillerymen standing on the parapets of the Algerian guns, as though shooing them away.

Miriam clutched Tommy to her chest, hunched her shoulders round him, and ran.

"Miss Albuyeh!" Lieutenant Saed called, clear of the crowd at last. "Where's the hurry? It could be hours. We have orders not to fire first!"

Just as the lieutenant finished speaking one of the shore batteries fired on *Queen Charlotte*. Two more guns discharged at the opposite end of the breakwater. Seconds later *Queen Charlotte's* full broadside roared out, followed by those of the anchored fleet training their guns on the City's fortifications. Miriam didn't stop running. Behind her on the quay was din, carnage, and hell-fire.

When a cannonball stuck in the thick outer wall surrounding the Consul's residence, Miriam went out to examine it. From her vantage point outside the villa walls she viewed the Algerian ships all ablaze in the harbor. Had the ships not been on fire it would have been difficult to distinguish anything in the bay, the bombardment had been going on for three hours. What was most visible at this distance were the tops of *Queen Charlotte's* masts, rising above a layer of smoke and dust thrown up from the destroyed batteries.

"A near run thing, Corporal," she said to the only remaining Algerian soldier at the Consul's villa, by way of comment on the shot.

Several areas of the City were burning. Miriam stared toward the fires, standing with the corporal at the door of the villa. The young soldier in his neat uniform shuffled, and patted the sword hanging from his sash, as though marching in place. Miriam wondered if he might live in a part of the City now ablaze.

Atif Mehmood came puffing up the twilit lane. "Take me to the house where the British are held, the useful ones, the surgeon is who we want. God be with you, Miss." Breathing heavily from his trek through the ancient tiered streets, he bowed to Miriam.

"The defense goes badly then," the young corporal said. "So many are wounded?"

"Hah! as to that, do not presume to question. Captain Ansari sends for the surgeon, that is all you need to know." Atif Mehmood caught Miriam's eye. "I daresay we have killed many pork and beef fed Englishmen today. Six hundred and more. Enough to fill one of their largest ships."

The head cook gave her a nod of satisfaction, and Miriam tried to appear suitably impressed.

"What are you waiting for?" Atif Mehmood said.

"Am I to leave my post then?" the corporal squeaked.

"Is the English lord not shackled within?"

"He is, but—"

"Leave your keys with this young woman, and come along at once. Was she not sent by the Dey Himself to look after the infidel's young? They are not capable of it themselves. You shall return to your post directly we deliver the physician."

With a look of relief the corporal gave his keys into Miriam's hand. She noted the direction they set off, and their first turning. When they were out of sight, she ran into the villa and emerged again draped in a black head scarf.

Miriam returned to the Consul's residence as swiftly as she could after following Atif Mehmood and the corporal to the house, a few streets away, where *Prometheus's* people were held. The guard there was light. If the good British tars within knew there were but two men standing sentry, there would have been a dust up. Atif Mehmood and the corporal took the precaution of bundling the surgeon away with a length of turban cloth tied about his eyes. Even over the boom of the great guns—a background din that seemed as if it had always been there, so long had it gone on—Miriam heard Tommy's shrieking.

She sped toward the sound and found Tommy with one of the kitchen servants.

"Be so good as to give the child his milk," Miriam said. "I have matters to attend to with the British Consul." She strode out of the cook house, the haughty *hanim*.

"Oh, Miriam! May I call you Miriam?" Lord Elgin cried.

Miriam entered meaning to unlock his manacles, but instead she dropped the key she'd been clutching into her pocket. He was unharmed, Lieutenant Saed having done him the courtesy of shackling his hands in front of him. An active man could have done much left in that position.

"If I only knew how the battle goes on!" Lord Elgin said. "At least tell me what you can make out from the window, dear girl."

She moved obligingly to the window, but as they were on the ground floor and a high wall surrounded the villa, there was only the garden to be seen.

"Earlier I saw the City on fire, my lord, at least three separate blazes. And there is such a prodigious quantity of smoke in the harbor, I make no doubt your forces will have destroyed the Dey's entire fleet."

"To say nothing of the batteries guarding the breakwater," Lord Elgin said. "And the guns protecting the City."

"The great guns have been firing on Algiers since three o'clock this afternoon."

"Oh yes." Lord Elgin lifted his manacled hands as though it were not obvious he was chained in place. "They may prevent me from taking an active part in this battle, but I have studied martial tactics and I can imagine how it has gone. Lord Exmouth and the force from Gibraltar will by this time have destroyed not only the Dey's entire fleet, but the greater part of the batteries protecting the anchorage and the City. I heard what I take to be rockets. Those are the cause of the fires you saw in the City. I would wager the fires shall soon spread to the store houses, and have all the commerce near the quay ablaze."

"With the loss of thousands of lives," Miriam said, "and the expense of how many million sequins."

She stared at Lord Elgin. He was a diplomat sent to pursue the interests of the Crown above all else to be sure, but had he no fellow feeling for the people he'd lived among? Miriam withdrew her hand entirely from the pocket of her dress. She'd best remember why she was there, and stop making out that people were any better than they were. Miriam forced a smile onto her face, to take the bite out of her last words.

Lord Elgin rubbed his hands together, clanking the chain that bound his manacles to an anvil on the floor. "I must thank you for your part in helping Lady Elgin and Fanny get away."

"I could wish your dear little boy had gotten away too, but babies will cry. It's what they do, and I must go see he has taken his milk."

Miriam moved toward the drawing room door.

"A moment, if you please, Miriam," Lord Elgin said. "You will not forget there is another helpless sufferer under this roof, I trust? Be a good girl, and see if you can smuggle past the guards a bottle of the Haut Brion with the long cork and perhaps a pye. That fat cook makes a fine sea pye."

She turned to Lord Elgin slowly, to look the man in the face who would be feasting while countrymen died.

"I shall try my very best, your lordship." Miriam averted her gaze in a diffident way before continuing, "May I ask a favor of you, sir, in return? You see I came to you from Lord Q with only the clothes I stand up in. May I...that is, might I have your permission to make free of Lady Elgin's or Miss Fanny's wardrobe?"

She finished her appeal in a small voice, and peeked at Lord Elgin through her lashes. Miriam caught the look of utter relief on his face, which was quickly followed by a smug expression that seemed to proclaim just how well he understood women.

"My dear girl! Of course, you must make free of my wife's wardrobe, and her daughter's if you so choose. I daresay Fanny's things will suit you better. You are a mere slip of a—"

"I am very much obliged to you," Miriam broke in, to prevent him calling her girl one more time. False gratitude, it turned out, tasted bitter.

She dropped a hasty curtsey and fled the presence of the British Consul to Algiers.

CHAPTER THREE

"H.M.S. Queen Charlotte
Algiers Bay, August 20, 18XX

Sir, - For your atrocities at Bona on defenceless Christians, and your unbecoming disregard to the demands I made yesterday, in the name of the Prince Regent of England, the fleet under my orders has given you signal chastisement by the total destruction of your navy, storehouse, and arsenal, with half your batteries.

As England does not war for the destruction of cities, I am unwilling to visit your personal cruelties upon the inoffensive inhabitants of the country, and I therefore offer you the same terms of peace which I conveyed to you yesterday in my sovereign's name; without the acceptance of those terms you can have no peace with England.

If you receive this offer as you ought, you will fire three guns, and I shall consider your not making this signal as a refusal, and shall renew my operations at my own convenience.

I offer you the above terms *provided* neither the British Consul, nor the officers and men, so wickedly seized by you from the boats of a British ship of war, have met with any cruel treatment, or any of the Christian slaves in your power; and I repeat my demand, that the Consul, officers, and men may be sent off to me conformably to ancient treaties.

I have, etc.,
Exmouth"

At first light Miriam crept into the small sitting room where Lord Elgin was asleep, drooling on his shirt front, and woke and unshackled him. By nine o'clock that morning the Consul's villa was filled with British sea officers, marines, and a contingent of rough pigtailed seamen. In a nondescript gray morning dress, with a black scarf covering her head and shoulders as before, Miriam led Mr. Burgess and his men to the house where *Prometheus's* people remained, unguarded.

She hurried alone back to Lord Elgin's villa. The neighborhood, a part of the City dedicated to foreigners, was deserted and still except for the houses occupied by the British. Enough noise to fill the entire quarter began to issue from those two residences.

Red and blue jackets crowded every ground floor hallway and apartment of the Consul's villa. Miriam slipped through into an upstairs servant's bedchamber where she'd left her basket and spare dress, and all the finery she'd looted from Lady Elgin and Miss Fanny's wardrobes. Through the window of her chamber, Miriam watched a group of seamen running up the lane, several taking the place of a horse between the traces of a curricle.

She frowned and backed out of view. Miriam wanted to curl up on the narrow bed in the chamber, to awaken later and creep away unnoticed clad in the *burqa*. But the mission wasn't played out, and without it concluding successfully, Miriam might lose the small British support she had at present. She set to the task of tarting up—fit to ride to the quay in a curricle pulled by British tars.

Miriam turned many heads, truthfully every head, when she sprang her presence on the group of sea officers and marines gathered with Lord Elgin in the great room of the manse. Sweeping in wearing a cunning mixture of Fanny's more demure girlish gown and Lady Elgin's scarves and embellishments, she was the picture of aristocratic elegance, from her satin pumps to the fringes of her ridiculously large hat and parasol. Miriam moved immediately to take up Tommy from where he lay on a sofa, forgotten by all but a hard faced sergeant who was allowing the child to suck his knuckle.

A renewed and louder stir broke out in the room, immediately filling the silence created by Miriam's entrance. They were apparently waiting for nothing more than her appearance. The crowd carried Miriam, Tommy, and Lord Elgin outside and installed them in the man-drawn curricle. Miriam settled on the bench seat with Tommy against her, managing to free both hands for an instant to open her parasol. She needed it as a shield against the humiliation of being paraded through the blown out City in that absurd conveyance, surrounded by hallooing British men.

Miriam sat with her back straight, and what she hoped were haughty, insensible, composed features. Inwardly she shrank, both from making a spectacle of herself, and from the appearance of indifference to the suffering of others. To the credit of lieutenant Burgess and the British tars the outcry became much less as they neared the quay, and passed through the areas hardest hit in the battle. First down side streets and then on the main thoroughfare itself corpses appeared, and torn body parts. Filthy, bloody, lying in the street. This was the aftermath of victory.

Lord Elgin, Miriam, and Tommy where obliged to get down from the curricle before reaching the quay, because of the great crowd gathering there, just as on the previous day. Today freed Christian slaves, many ragged and dirty, others more decently treated, clothed and fed, were being herded about by the British. As Miriam adjusted Tommy against her shoulder she glanced back the way they'd come, and spotted—she didn't think she could be mistaken—the portly figure of Atif Mehmood supporting Captain Ansari up the road. Behind them they left the bodies of their comrades, many draped over the ruined gun embrasures. Captain Ansari, lifting a head wrapped in a disarrayed and bloody turban, gazed back at the scene of disaster. Miriam turned and put up her parasol with a nonchalant air.

A number of carriages were drawn up at the entrance of the quay. Their occupants, the surviving quality of the City, were watching the spectacle of exodus from the comfort of their barouches. Miriam heard 'Lord and Lady Elgin' whispered as they passed. The gown, the unwieldy parasol, and extravagant hat had done their duty.

Miriam felt unexpected relief at sight of the young captain she'd met on the quay, coming forward to greet Mr. Burgess and Lord Elgin and his party.

"Lord Elgin, I am Captain Dashwood. How do you do, sir? Lord Exmouth sends his best compliments, and Mr. Burgess and his lordship's barge to carry you aboard *Queen Charlotte*. The lady will be doing me the honour of her presence aboard *Prometheus*, by his lordship's order."

Lord Elgin received this news with indifference, made a curt bow to Miriam, and asked to be shown to the barge. Miriam turned frantically round, and spotting the rough-hewn sergeant of the sucked on digit, she gave Tommy a fond kiss and embrace and handed him into the man's arms. When Tommy realized he was to part from Miriam, with whom he'd come to associate some minimal level of comfort, he began to howl.

"Bear up, my boy," Lord Elgin advised him from his seat in the stern of the barge. "You are to see your mama, in the time it takes to pull to the flag."

With a stricken wail Tommy held out his arms to Miriam. Captain Dashwood escorted Miriam away to *Prometheus's* boat, with many a sidelong glance at her costume and unveiled face. Getting into the gig almost undid Miriam for she was obliged, before Captain Dashwood and his men, to remove her satin pumps. These she placed in the basket with her belongings. Captain Dashwood seated himself in the stern of the boat beside her, and gave the order to "pull away".

Miriam's stomach lifted and fell with the send of the sea passing under the boat's bow. She'd accomplished what the British asked of her in exchange for her safe passage out of Iran. Whether this cancelled her indebtedness, she did not know. And if it did, where was she to go with never a friend in the world? Anxiety gnawed at her, almost outweighing her relief and fatigue.

It spite of weariness—Miriam's head was threatening to loll forward onto her breast—she untied one of the sashes from round her waist and arranged it over her hair, fastening it about her neck and shoulders in the manner of a *hijab*. She wanted to go aboard *Prometheus*, into that all male world, with an appearance of decency.

In the two days following the bombardment of Algiers, Lord Exmouth and the Dutch commander Vice-Admiral Baron Van der Capellen contemplated their losses, repaired their ships, and arranged transport for the eventual three thousand Christian slaves freed. Between the British and Dutch forces one hundred thirty men were killed and seven hundred wounded. Word from *Prometheus's* surgeon and others who'd been pressed into aiding the enemy with their casualties, put the Algerian losses in the thousands of men dead and wounded. Lord Exmouth was fortunate in losing no ships, though some had sustained the cannonading of the shore batteries for long periods and been severely damaged.

Captain Dashwood with *Prometheus* and other ships of the fleet towed and lent aid to both British and Dutch ships. In spite of the high pitch of activity during those two days, Dashwood missed the presence of his lady guest. Miss Kodio Blackwell kept her apartment, the coach was converted to a bed place for her use. On the third day, Dashwood had an excuse to send his steward scratching on her door. A boat from the flag brought a letter requesting and requiring *Prometheus's* captain to receive Admiral Lord Exmouth aboard for supper that evening.

It was difficult to choose between Dashwood and Miriam which was the more disturbed in spirit before this meeting, as they awaited the Admiral's appearance in *Prometheus's* great cabin. They exhausted their small store of conversation in greetings and polite inquiries as to how the other did. Miriam sat outwardly composed but silent. Her hands were clasped in her lap as she gazed out the stern windows at the lights of the ship anchored nearest. Dashwood paced up and back in the small space, stopping abruptly now and again as though he would speak to her. He actually gave a skip and jump in the air when his steward knocked on the door "to alert his honor the Admiral's barge was alongside."

Dashwood ran out the door, clapping his hat to his head as he went. Miriam stood, heaved a sigh, and smoothed her gown with shaking hands. There was a great noise above her head, the shrilling of a pipe, the stamp of feet planted on the deck in unison. Moments later Lord Exmouth came sweeping into the great cabin, ducking his head, followed by Dashwood with his hat once more under his arm.

"How do you do, Miss Miriam?" His lordship and Miriam were previously acquainted, and he immediately came and took Miriam's hand. "I must caution you not to lie, for Valentine already told me you were obliged to keep your bed these last days."

Miriam was taken aback, but she looked straight at Lord Exmouth and answered him directly. "I'm very well, sir, I thank you. I won't deny then, that I was in need of a good rest, which...Captain Valentine Dashwood has kindly allowed me."

Lord Exmouth turned to Dashwood with a smile and a nod as though to say, 'Didn't I tell you the girl had bottom.'

"Do be seated," Lord Exmouth said, and planted his rather grand, stout, and well dressed person knee to knee with

Miriam. "I must beg your pardon for not receiving you as you deserve, aboard *Queen Charlotte*. I regret to say there are certain uninformed parties aboard my ship at present, crying out about 'wicked nurses', who've misunderstood your...er, role in what has occurred in these last days."

"Just as they ought," Miriam said.

Lord Exmouth's genial open face broke into a huge grin, and he even gave a small snort. "But I daresay the party's enmity may have more to do with the world's exclaiming how well Lady Elgin looked as she came away. Like a heroine, on her lord's arm after the battle."

Miriam frowned and glanced down, while the smile slowly faded from Lord Exmouth's face. Lord Exmouth covered his confusion with a little cough; Dashwood shifted in his chair.

"And how does Miss Fanny and dear little Tommy do?"

"Very well, ma'am," Lord Exmouth said, in a hardy, relieved tone. "Miss Fanny is the belle of my flag captain's table. And as Tommy has no nurse, he has been given in charge to Jemmy Ducks."

"How glad I am to hear it." Miriam smiled for the first time. "And who is this Jemmy Ducks?"

Lord Exmouth's face glowed pink with pleasure. "You tell her Dashwood, it's too rich."

Dashwood hesitated as though he wanted to refuse, but of course as an officer, a much junior officer, he could not. "Well ma'am, in the Navy, Jemmy Ducks is the name we give the seaman in charge of the poultry, and the pigs."

A great quantity of pork was served at supper, to which the gentlemen at least did justice, along with several bottles of wine. Dashwood was sensitive to what he thought were Miriam's religious dictates, and had his cook prepare a fowl in oyster sauce especially for her. Miriam also recognized upon the table a dish containing the oysters preserved in peppered oil that she'd purchased at the *souk* in Algiers. These Miriam spooned onto her plate with relish, while she observed the gentlemen. They were already jovial, especially Lord Exmouth with his mirth all out of proportion to the deserts of that Jemmy Ducks sally. Miriam watched them grow more lively with each empty bottle that was carried away into the pantry.

Yet when the covers were drawn and the port and almonds were on the table, Lord Exmouth grew serious and turned pointedly to her.

"Miss Miriam, you have done your part most admirably. Anyone intimate in this Algiers affair knows it. Lord Q has certainly been made aware of your..."

His lordship stopped speaking suddenly, and cocked his ear at the sound of a marine on *Prometheus's* deck hailing an approaching boat.

"We are to be joined shortly, ma'am, by the commander of the Dutch fleet, Baron Van der Capellen, so I must be brief." Lord Exmouth paused, gave an awkward twist of neck and head, and loosened his stock with two meaty fingers. "A matter has arisen that we, that is Lord Q feels will be best addressed by someone with your particular, ah, assets. That is, by a woman."

The bosun's pipe shrilled and the two Navy men jumped to their feet, made hasty bows to Miriam, and hurried up on deck.

Miriam was expecting to learn of her fate this evening, and naturally she'd played over in her mind what the English might do with her. The most likely scenario was that she should be packed off to be governess to some British diplomat's children. There were many who would say it was what she'd been raised for, that or to be the wife of a diplomat or minor official. Miriam's step-father, Francis Blackwell, had given her an education in geography, languages, history, and made her unfit for many other ways of life. But she'd hardly imagined that the British, that Lord Q, should wish to make use of her assets...as a woman. She was rather chilled by the prospect.

Baron Van der Capellen was shown in to the cabin by Dashwood, with Lord Exmouth behind him, and presented to Miriam. Van der Capellen was a ponderous, florid man, with a careworn face. After they were seated again, he peered at Miriam in a short sighted way, and eased a gold oval shaped locket out of a waistcoat pocket stretched tight across his belly. Van der Capellen flicked open the lid to reveal a small portrait and placed the locket on the table before them.

"This is a likeness of my niece, Anna Lovell, Miss Blackwell," Van der Capellen said, in the direct way of Navy men. "My favorite niece, I hasten to add, daughter of my dearest sister. Anna was on her way aboard the merchant vessel *Vriendschap*, from the island of Hong Kong to Java, to marry the captain of *Dageraad*. This merchantman was attacked, Miss, by foul pirates in the South China Sea. Our dear Anna was taken from us."

Tears welled in Van der Capellen's eyes and he nodded toward Lord Exmouth, who cleared his throat.

"We've known of these activities for some time, reports come to us from Hong Kong and Malaya of merchant ships and private vessels seized and robbed. The passengers subjected to beatings and indignities..." Lord Exmouth broke off, realizing late he was most probably giving pain to the Dutch Vice-Admiral. "And in short, this time they've gone too far, and Government has become involved."

Miriam saw how it was, this time the pirates took a woman about whom someone cared, a light-skinned woman, a privileged European woman. Or at least a well-connected one, and Miriam knew the British were indebted to the Dutch for their support in the late battle. What Miriam also guessed at was Lord Q's plan, that she should help retire that debt, and her own, by venturing into the South China Sea.

"What if I do not wish, your lordship," Miriam said to Lord Exmouth, "to become involved along with Government, to make a perilous journey so far East?"

"Why then, Miss Miriam, you should be instantly put ashore. Or passage can be arranged for you back to Iran. It would be your choice."

The alacrity with which this answer shot back at her from the genial Lord Exmouth, and the somewhat hard stare that accompanied it, surprised Miriam. Van der Capellen, and Dashwood too, if she was not mistaken, were avoiding her eye.

"Then I had better learn the extent that your government is involved, sir, and all the particulars of the case." Miriam turned to Van der Capellen. She took up the portrait of Anna Lovell—a delicate painting on ivory—and really looked at the pale skinned, rosy checked, fair-haired maid with the upturned nose. "I'm sorry for your niece, sir, I shall do everything I can to aid her."

"Oh!" cried Baron Van der Capellen, clasping Miriam's hand holding the portrait. "May God speed you." The Dutch Vice-Admiral's gaze left her and sought Lord Exmouth. "And bless the Royal Navy."

Baron Van der Capellen had left them. In the cabin Lord Exmouth, Captain Dashwood, and Miriam bent over a map of the South China Sea.

"I do not see how we are to find a single ship in an area of this size," Miriam observed. "Even were the Navy to send a fleet."

"Give Lord Q some credit, Miss Miriam. We know the name of the vessel that kidnapped Miss Lovell. The *Golden Dragon*, she is called. And a scourge she has been to our merchant fleet, and maritime trade in those waters. It is past time something were done to bring those savages to heel."

Lord Exmouth paused, but as the remark found no favor with Miriam, he continued, "Lord Q's people mapped the *Dragon's* preferred hunting grounds and routes of attack."

Miriam couldn't suppress a small shudder, knowing she was to be the prey sent in to those hunting grounds. Yet she wasn't completely ignorant of world geography, and remained unconvinced the British had a viable plan.

"Another question that strikes me most forcefully, your lordship," she said, "is whether there will be any hope of finding Miss Lovell after the months it will require to reach the South China Sea. I do not wish to bring any ill on the poor woman by speaking this aloud, but will she not have been moved on to the mainland of China, by the time I can expect to arrive?"

Captain Dashwood shivered but Lord Exmouth wasn't the least disturbed.

His lordship paused, allowing a dramatic beat to pass. "You shall be put aboard a crack ship, Miss Miriam."

Whatever this meant, it made Captain Dashwood gasp.

Lord Exmouth nodded with satisfaction. "*Nonesuch*, Captain Maximus Thorpe, is expected in Algiers. You shall be put aboard her, and Captain Thorpe will be apprised he is to deliver you to Hong Kong with due dispatch, wasting not a moment. Once in Hong Kong you will meet with the diplomatic corps. One of the local people will attend you, someone with whom you are already acquainted." Lord Exmouth gave Miriam a significant and considering stare. "It is Mr. Francis Blackwell, Miss Miriam. Did you know he was posted in Hong Kong?"

This news gave Miriam a start, but she refrained from gasping with an effort. "I was not, sir." She knew Francis was one of Lord Q's people, as his lordship called them, though she must never admit it. "But that is not an issue in the least."

"From Hong Kong you will proceed to Java," Lord Exmouth said, "in vessels and under terms you will know best how to arrange, Miss Miriam. In the same brilliant fashion you have done here in Algiers, no doubt."

Miriam had many doubts about the mission, but she acknowledged Lord Exmouth's compliment with a graceful inclination of her head. A crack ship not withstanding, she couldn't imagine being in time to save Miss Lovell from sale in the slave trade. But to disrupt or ruin the trafficking would be a great good to other women, and this there might yet be a chance of doing. The entire scheme, and thoughts of meeting Francis again, whirled about in Miriam's head. She wanted to be alone, to work out how she felt. Was she more relieved or terrified for her immediate future?

"You and Baron Van der Capellen have put into my hands a great trust, and given me much to consider. I am obliged to you for that confidence, Lord Exmouth. And thank you, Captain Dashwood, for the excellent supper and hospitality. Though I have questions yet, I believe I shall reserve them and retire. The better to think on what I need to know."

Both gentlemen stood up.

"Good night, Miss Miriam, and God bless," his lordship said, an affectionate sparkle in his eyes. "Is there anything you could wish for, either pertaining to to-night's discussion or otherwise?"

Miriam took a moment to consider. "A Chinese scholar, sir, or someone to educate me in the Malay and Eastern languages—of which I am completely ignorant."

"That, Dashwood," said Lord Exmouth, after they had bowed Miriam out of the great cabin, "is quite a girl."

They were distantly related on Dashwood's mother's side. It was not much of a connection, yet enough for Dashwood to be considered a fortunate son in the Navy, where influence was concerned.

"Woman, sir, I think you mean," said Dashwood, in a distracted tone. "I'd like a private word, sir, if I may. Before your barge is called."

Lord Exmouth sat down with a little harrumph, the older generation cannot like being brought up by the younger.

"I know what you will say, that it is a deuced ugly thing to pitch a girl, er, woman like that, in among savages and pirates."

"No, sir, that is not what I was going to say, though it is a fine point come to think of it." Dashwood frowned and pursed his lips. "What I wanted to speak of is my desire, my long hoped for chance, to be posted aboard the crack ship."

"Valentine, you astonish me! Are you so much in love with her already, that you would follow her into a crack ship? Where you would be a mere lieutenant again, let me remind you."

An exasperated expression passed over Dashwood's face, those of Lord Exmouth's generation really were a romantic set of beings. He pitched his voice low. "Sir, Miss Blackwell is a remarkable woman, and not unblessed with the charms of the fair sex to a great degree, but I haven't known her near long enough to form an attachment. I regret to say my request is purely a selfish one. It has always been the greatest desire of my heart to serve aboard a crack ship."

Lord Exmouth leaned back, staring in amazement. "Really, you cannot have thought this through, and as your mother's second cousin's cousin I feel it my duty to tell you so. You are a well-looking man, fit, young, your whole career ahead of you. Would you exchange all that for a few years of glory?" Lord Exmouth paused, and took a great swallow of his port. "I was not accounted timid in my day, not behindhand in the way of taking prizes and harrying the French, but I should have hesitated, I should have hesitated very much indeed before putting myself in an air-ship."

"It is a modern, more scientific Service today, Sir, if I may be so bold," Dashwood said. "One in which I hope to find the rewards more than compensation for the danger to life and limb. As I told you, sir, it has been the greatest desire of my heart since ever so long ago."

"Long ago, is it?" Lord Exmouth grumbled. "And you such an oldster, Dashwood. Well, this discussion is neither here nor there. If you know about crack ships, you will understand they are somewhat autonomous vessels, loosely under Admiralty and Lord Q's control. A crack ship's captain has the final decision of who he will take aboard his ship, the risks being what they are, and I can do no more than suggest—"

"Oh, Sir!" Dashwood cried. "Thank you very much, sir."

"Do not thank me, if you please. I cannot feel that I will be doing you any great turn by putting you in Maximus Thorpe's way. Wait until you meet Captain Thorpe, then decide how much it is your heart's desire to be aboard a crack ship. Some call him crack-headed, and most agree he is a frightening beast on his best days."

The ship heeled and creaked, straining at her anchor with the wind in the West. Dashwood grasped the edge of the table. "Can it be right to send Miss Blackwell under the protection of such a person?"

"Right? There is nothing right about this business, and as far as delivering Miss Miriam to the scene of action, what choice do we have? In any case, I am not concerned about Captain Thorpe's acceptance of our young lady aboard the *Nonesuch*. He is a man, after all, and she is...not without charms. I more than half suspicion, your protests notwithstanding, that this desire of your heart to be aboard a crack ship has to do with that charmer, and I am here to tell you it will not do. Miss Miriam Kodio Blackwell was raised in a seraglio, she is a Muslim. She is not one of us."

Lying in an officer's cot in the coach, with only thin pine boards separating Miriam's apartment from the great cabin, she heard every word of the gentlemen's conversation. In this second hand way Miriam learned more of her fate and future. What she'd done for Lord and Lady Elgin had not been enough, not nearly enough to be sent to England to take up a respectable quiet life. Miriam admitted to a certain feeling of relief on that score, on any number of others her mind was anything but easy.

One cause of unease was this crack ship, that the Navy men spoke of in such odd terms, and her equally extraordinary captain. The mission in the South China Sea Miriam avoided considering too deeply, it being at such a distance and the thought of putting herself into pirates' hands so foreign and appalling. She was infinitely glad to have requested a Chinese teacher. A woman had mainly her wits to protect her, and it was hard to be witty without language. But learning she should be considered no fit match for a man like Captain Valentine Dashwood hurt her, as did admitting she cared about it at all. It kept her from sleeping. How long was she to be part of them, and not one of us?

CHAPTER FOUR

Captain Maximus Thorpe stood on the quarterdeck of His Majesty's Hired Vessel *Nonesuch* with the late afternoon sun in his face, hands clasped behind his back and feet planted apart, watching the approach of Admiral Lord Exmouth's barge. Sir Edward Pellew had called upon Maximus the evening before, almost as soon as *Nonesuch* hove to in the Bay of Algiers, rather than making the ship's number and summoning her captain aboard the flag. In the breast pocket of Maximus's jacket was the letter from Lord Q that Sir Edward brought him, requesting and requiring Maximus to take on board *Nonesuch* three individuals who were, to his way of thinking, questionable characters.

The lieutenant he would almost certainly accept, the ship being down to one officer. Mr. Hermes Dodd, the officer of the watch, stood not far from Maximus, glaring at the barge through slitted eyes. *Nonesuch's* first officer had dropped out during the last cruise, a hazard peculiar to crack ships. But a hoyden, a preening female agent of Lord Q's he would not have aboard his ship, and so he'd told Sir Edward the evening before. His lordship returned him a sly, knowing smile that rather disconcerted Maximus, though he'd not let the smug Sir Edward see it. The China scholar, of course, went as a pair with the female, so if he was not to have one, he would not be burdened with either.

"In the case where you will allow aboard the young Miss," Sir Edward said, "and in responding to this Code Black, gratify Lord Q as well as ensure cordial relations with our allies the Dutch, should you prefer the scholar be a seaman as well?"

"Eh?" Maximus was struck by Sir Edward's coolness, his assumption. "What do you mean?"

"Should you prefer a lascar, or a dyak? A man thoroughly familiar with the sea and a ship's business, as well as the languages of the far East?"

Mr. Dodd stepped toward Maximus, recalling him from his reverie. "Now, sir?"

Maximum nodded. Mr. Dodd called out. "Boat ahoy! What boat is that?"

"*Queen Charlotte!*" came the immediate reply.

Maximus gave the necessary orders, and the bosun took up his station prepared to pipe the Admiral aboard. There were neither marines nor young gentlemen aboard *Nonesuch,* no sideboys in white gloves or smart looking soldiers. His crew was in attendance on deck, looking neither smart nor particularly white.

Lord Exmouth came aboard, followed by a sprightly young fellow who fairly leapt on the deck. No Merry Andrews, if you please, Maximus thought. And then the female was handed up, and all other considerations fled from his mind. Astounded, Maximus came forward and exchanged salutes and handshakes with the officers.

"Captain Thorpe," Sir Edward said, "may I present Miss Miriam Albuyeh Kodio Blackwell. Miss Miriam, Captain Maximus Thorpe."

"Servant, ma'am," Maximus managed. With one last glance round the deck of *Nonesuch* and the surrounding sea, where ash and debris from the battle still floated in a sad and dirty scum, he invited his guests below to the great cabin.

What struck Maximus was how much this young woman was the opposite of his expectation. She was clad in a plain gray morning gown, a neat trim little person no more than a decade his junior, with a shawl completely covering her hair. It was the shawl draped over her head in that manner, shielding her face from scrutiny, that reminded Maximus so forcefully of the countrywomen of his native Scotland. He felt almost tongue-tied before her. Miss Miriam Albuyeh Kodio Blackwell was no more a hoyden than Maximus himself was a cur.

In the great cabin, Sir Edward stood rubbing his hands together in delighted fashion. Maximus ushered them to seats on chairs or stern lockers.

"Saramago!" Maximus shouted to this steward. "Wine and cake, if you please."

The young lady was startled by his calling out.

"Forgive me, Miss Albu...ah, Kodio, that is to say Blackwell?"

"Perhaps it would be simplest if you called me Miss Miriam, sir." She'd pushed back her head scarf on entering the cabin, so that a ring of brilliant black hair framed her face. "As his lordship and Captain Dashwood do."

"Aye, well, ah, how kind, Miss Miriam. Welcome aboard *Nonesuch*, ma'am, that is all I wished to say."

Sir Edward chuckled aloud, and while Maximus tried to glare him down, the young spark Dashwood leaped into the breach.

"You will forgive me, I hope, Miss Miriam, if I speak out of turn. But it is no longer Captain Dashwood. Since leaving *Prometheus* I am plain Mr. Dashwood again. Happily so, if Captain Thorpe will have me aboard."

Dashwood blushed at that last, as well he might.

At least this put Maximus into known waters. "As it transpires, Mr. Dashwood, *Nonesuch* is in need of a lieutenant. Your service in *Prometheus* and elsewhere, I had your detailed history from his lordship I may assure you, speaks well for you. Yet all your fine experience may not fit you for service in a crack ship."

"Sir, I attended all Doctor John Herschel's lectures at the Royal Astronomical Society, and studied the catalogues of double stars by him and his honored father. It has always been the sincerest desire of my heart to serve aboard an air—"

"Yes, Mr. Dashwood, I heard about the wishes of your heart at length as well, I thank you. I hope you will be allowing me to pose what may appear an unseemly set of questions, so I may better judge your fitness for service."

Maximus frowned as his steward, Saramago, entered the cabin with the side tassels of his ever present knitted cap swinging. Saramago set the refreshments down on the table, stole a glance at the young lady, and grinning in a way that revealed more gum than tooth he slipped away.

"Miss Miriam," Maximus said, "in the questions I put to Mr. Dashwood, I hope you will think on your own history and speak up if you can answer aye to any of them." Maximus wished she might not consider him indelicate, about his crew he had no hopes. "Now Mr. Dashwood, do you or does anyone in your family, most particularly a mother or father, suffer from apoplexies, vapors, flutterings, or irregular rhythms of the heart?"

"No, sir, not that I am aware."

"Do you feel nauseated, when in the topgallant crosstrees? You served in *Ganges*, Mr. Dashwood, a 98-gun ship. When in her foremast topgallant crosstrees, let us say? And ma'am, if you were ever on a summit of great height?"

"No, sir," Dashwood said.

"No, sir," Miriam echoed. Her eyes gleamed with lively interest, as though she'd questions of her own, but good manners kept her silent.

"Well, then, that is a start." Maximus clapped his hands down on his knees. "Very well, indeed. We shall finish our wine, and then I will show you both round the ship. After which, Mr. Dashwood, I'm sure you will be wanting to change into working clothes, and make yourself known to Mr. Dodd."

"Oh, sir!" Dashwood cried. "Aye, aye, sir. Thank you, sir."

"Mr. Dashwood, I find I have to take you on as first lieutenant, but I tell you this frankly and before his lordship, that if I had my way Mr. Dodd would be first lieutenant and you the junior. By which I mean no disrespect to you, no far from it, it is only that Mr. Dodd has served in *Nonesuch* three years. A considerable time in a crack ship."

"Mr. Dodd will have much valuable knowledge, sir," Dashwood said, "that I hope he will share with me."

Maximus smiled. "That attitude does you great credit, Mr. Dashwood. Ma'am, if you are quite ready let us begin our inspection."

Mr. Dashwood jumped up with alacrity at the invitation to tour the ship, but Lord Exmouth begged to be excused. Moving through the cramped between decks, where she could mostly stand upright but the men could not, Miriam understood why Lord Exmouth shouldn't wish to squeeze his bulk through the—to him—familiar innards of a small ship of war.

The odd Captain Thorpe, whose appearance at first surprised and almost frightened Miriam, led them through the officers' quarters, the gun room, and then down a ladder stair to a lower tier where rested the great smelly anchor cables of the ship. Captain Thorpe and Mr. Dashwood walked rapidly back and forth, Miriam trailing them, talking of proper stowage of flotation, ballast, and trim.

The officers sent Miriam first up the ladder to the deck they'd just quitted, averting their eyes as she climbed. Captain Thorpe led them forward past where Miriam knew a row of cannons should have been. In this vessel there were gun ports but no great guns. There were seamen about, the off watch below, who fell back out of Captain Thorpe's path, knuckling their foreheads.

Miriam tried not to appear too much agog. In the same way some girls were fascinated by horses growing up, she'd been in love with ships and read all she could about matters maritime. Consequently Miriam was deeply curious about *Nonesuch's* differences from other vessels, but she would never make herself conspicuous by vulgar questioning of the Captain.

One of the greatest oddities about *Nonesuch*, Miriam couldn't help but notice, was how many of her crew were missing fingers, and more disconcerting, parts of their noses. Some of the seamen had strapped to wrists or elbows strange leathern and metal appendages, pinchers, hooks, and claw like arrangements, where once had been a hand, fingers, or arm.

The men with disfigured faces, however, could do nothing about it, just as Captain Thorpe couldn't help the fact he had one brilliant green eye and one pale, washed out blue eye. The combination of those strange eyes and flame-colored hair gave Miriam something of a start. Like Judas Iscariot, was Miriam's initial thought. When she was ten she remembered the American woman Mercedes, who'd lived with them for a short time in the Dey of Oran's harem in Ceuta, telling her the Spanish believed the betrayer of their Lord had red hair.

Miriam fancied she was not squeamish, missish, or any of those ish's, nor was she ignorant of the world. She read Fanny Burney's *Evelina*, and knew all about the rough characters given seamen. This set of men though, were not a great number lame in some way? Miriam followed the tall frame and red hair of Captain Thorpe forward along the deck, shuddering ever so slightly. Glancing back at Mr. Dashwood, Miriam discovered, rather than showing apprehension at the state of his new crew, he was fairly dancing on his toes.

Captain Thorpe held back a heavy canvas curtain, and motioned them into the foremost part of the ship.

"This area of the ship is the cockpit, Miss Miriam," Captain Thorpe said, "where the wounded are treated in battle.

Except in a crack ship, where it is more the command center, just as the quarterdeck is to a frigate. With your leave, ma'am."

Captain Thorpe bowed, and then hastened over to prevent Mr. Dashwood upsetting a beautiful circular object set into a table in the manner of a globe, in such a way that its many discs could spin on various axis.

"A most beautiful piece...of art is it, Sir?" Miriam asked. Jewel like rounded balls dotted the face of one disc, suspended from its surface in concentric circles.

"It is a Mechanism," Mr. Dashwood breathed reverentially.

Captain Thorpe tugged at his stock and glanced sideways at Miriam. Giving a little ahem, he said, "The Mechanism is an ancient device, ma'am, of a particular nature to do with celestial positioning and weather prediction."

"These are the planets in the heavens." Mr. Dashwood pointed. "Do you see, Miss Miriam?"

"I should be most interested to understand its functioning."

"Mr. Dashwood," Captain Thorpe interposed, "may I call your attention to some of the other features of the cockpit?"

"By all means, Sir."

Miriam was left feeling snubbed, as Captain Thorpe led Mr. Dashwood round his command center. This was their professional world. She'd momentarily forgotten she had no place here, where she was decidedly not one of them.

All the way forward the men were discussing two oversized and heavily reinforced port hole windows, like great insect eyes, shuttered by wooden gun port lids.

"We unship them before ascension," Captain Thorpe said to Mr. Dashwood, "but when we are approaching port or with the Fleet, they are always down."

Captain Thorpe and Mr. Dashwood then turned to examining a series of complex lines and blocks running outwards from what Captain Thorpe called "the yoke". Miriam stood next to the Mechanism and, glancing at the beautiful object, found there was something odd about it that she couldn't quite name. Captain Thorpe was becoming enthused, seeming to have half forgot her presence. When the yoke was pulled up on, he explained, through the action of those lines and blocks, transmitted to the stunsails "set just so", the bow of the ship would rise. Miriam wondered whether she'd heard aright, and then it struck her what was different about the Mechanism.

The planets had changed positions from where they'd been before, when Miriam first approached it. This Mechanism was no ordinary ship's instrument. She hoped she wasn't caught gawping, because right then Captain Thorpe called to her.

"Ma'am, we are proceeding on deck." He turned to Mr. Dashwood. "A crack ship uses a prodigious quantity of canvas, booms, and spars. Admiral Lord Exmouth will no doubt oblige us with as much as he can spare."

In the open air on deck, Miriam gazed round on the ships of the fleet, beyond which rose the beautiful white walls of the City of Algiers, where here and there were seen burned out gaps like blackened teeth in an otherwise brilliant smile. The men set to a furious peering into the rigging, waving of arms, and discussion of wind direction and sailing qualities. Standing well back from them, Miriam studied her surroundings. It really was a small vessel, perhaps ninety feet in length, but by her three masts Miriam recognized her as a ship sloop. The seamen working on deck were less hideous than their brothers below, though there were eye patches, missing fingers, and no doubt toes by the way they limped. Miriam noticed again the lack of cannon, the guns lining the upper decks of the other ships nearby.

Captain Thorpe, returning with Mr. Dashwood to where Miriam stood near the mainmast, was saying, "We carry only swivels, bow and stern chasers, with special carriages so we can fix them amidships if needed. We strike them into the hold before getting underway in earnest. This being a short call for orders and, ah, passengers, I shall not bother swaying them up unless his lordship desires it."

"Oh!" Mr. Dashwood cried. "Miss Miriam, don't lean against that, I beg."

Miriam's sleeve was barely brushing the canvas covering over what she'd taken to be one or more of the ships' boats.

Captain Thorpe stepped forward, with a glance at Mr. Dashwood as though he were the ninny of the world, and offered Miriam his arm. "This way, if you please, ma'am. We should not keep his lordship waiting."

On the way back to the captain's quarters, Captain Thorpe pointed out the first lieutenant's cabin to Mr. Dashwood, with an encouraging word about shifting his fine rig for a working one. Since Captain Thorpe led the way he missed the glance exchanged by Miriam and Mr. Dashwood on parting, the near touch of hands that passed between them.

Inside the great cabin, Captain Thorpe and Miriam found that Lord Exmouth wasn't waiting alone. Before the Admiral stood a dark, narrow man, who upon their entrance immediately turned and made them a bow, pressing his palms together before his face. Miriam returned the bow with a polite and instant curtsey, while Captain Thorpe glared over her head at Sir Edward Pellew.

"Miss Miriam, allow me to present Mr. Boar...that is to say...seaman Boarhead."

The seaman dipped his head again to Miriam, this time facing her with a smile and a flash of black teeth.

Captain Thorpe was scowling mightily. Sir Edward hastened to fill the void of conversation. "Boarhead speaks a number of languages besides English, including Malay, the language of the Siamese, and several Far Eastern dialects, the Mandarin and Hindoo. And he can hand, reef, and steer."

Sir Edward smiled as though he thought his choice of China scholar unexceptionable.

"I am sure we shall do very well together," Miriam said.

"May I just have a word, Sir," Captain Thorpe said.

The captain and admiral moved away, leaving Miriam in Boarhead's company near the stern windows.

"May I trouble you again for your name?" Miriam said, in a low voice.

The dark man stood silent for several moments, then replied in an equally soft tone. "Jugma Bora, Miss, but it might be best to indulge the white man's odd humors. They are powerful and vengeful creatures."

Miriam clasped her hands together and said nothing more. On one side of her was the heated discussion taking place in hushed tones between Captain Thorpe and Lord Exmouth, and on the other the dark seaman with blackened teeth.

"If that is your idea of a China scholar, Sir Edward, I must say I am shocked at it. That man is a Dyak, all he lacks is the sharpened teeth. You would throw this boar's head at that young lady? Look at her."

Miriam stood with hands folded in front of her, mildly regarding the canvas covered deck.

"Pipe down, Maximus, he is the lesser of the evils I had at my disposal. The man is something of a prodigy with languages, and a thorough-going seaman."

"I don't recall insisting on that particular point, that was more your notion than mine." Captain Thorpe glared at Sir Edward. "I wonder at you Englishmen. Could you no find someone more gentleman-like to bring to Miss Miriam's notice? To say nothing of this unspeakable plan of Lord Q's to throw her into the way of—"

"You may stopper it right there. You and I are servants of the Crown—yes, you too sir, though you do not like to admit it—and as such we do as we are ordered. Government owes a debt of gratitude to the Dutch, and if it chooses to repay it in a way that may not be palatable to you and I, that is none of our concern."

"None of my concern, as captain of *Nonesuch*?"

"May I remind you," Sir Edward said, "and only the fact of our long association gives me the patience to do so, it is government funds his Majesty's Hired Vessel *Nonesuch*."

This was unanswerable, though both were aware a crack ship was a different animal.

"You may take satisfaction in the fact Miss Miriam shall be under your protection during the entirety of the voyage—may it not prove a long one." Sir Edward's voice took on a confidential tone. "She need never meet with Boarhead unless under your eye, if the idea offends you. Though I will caution you, as a friend, the same as I counseled young Dashwood. She is not one of us."

"I don't know what you can mean by that, Sir," Captain Thorpe replied coldly. Choosing to swallow down his anger, he stepped forward. "What is your name, mon? None of this boar's head nonsense."

"Jugma Bora, sir."

"Bora, you are dismissed. Report to first lieutenant Mr. Dashwood on deck. He and Mr. Dodd will assign you a division. You will be sent for, when you are wanted for...the language lessons."

Seaman Bora knuckled his forehead to Captain Thorpe. "Aye, aye, sir." The dark man made a deep bow to Miriam and Sir Edward, and left the cabin.

Captain Thorpe, Miriam, and Lord Exmouth were seated in the cabin. Lord Exmouth leaned toward Miriam.

"I must take leave of you, Miss Miriam," his lordship said. "I hope all the arrangements are to your satisfaction. I will repeat our Dutch friend Van der Capellen's wish to you of — Good God! What the devil, er, deuce is that?"

A tawny brown blur flew past his lordship's legs, and then an animal sat neatly on Miriam's lap regarding Lord Exmouth out of none too friendly deep amber colored eyes.

Captain Thorpe, who'd started back in his chair when the animal whisked by, said, "That, sir, begging your pardon, is a Thracian Hell-Cat. A gift of the Ottoman chief Megabazus. *Nonesuch's* last mission was to the Ionian, you will be remembering."

Miriam was stroking the Hell-Cat's head. It settled so that it could look at her, opening and then closing its eyes to slits in adoring fashion.

"It doesn't look so hellish to me, if I may say so." Miriam regarded the furry little creature with growing affection.

"The truth is, Miss Miriam," Captain Thorpe said, "this is the first I've seen of it since it was sent aboard. Where it hides itself I could not say, but there is nothing like the rat population aboard we've had in former times."

Lord Exmouth sniffed. "Take your opportunity to put it ashore, that's my advice. They are dangerous creatures, are they not?"

"Dangerous, rare, independent creatures," Captain Thorpe said.

"Admirable qualities, in my view." Miriam pinned the cat's ears against its head with her caresses.

"What you can want with such an unnatural beast aboard an equally dangerous—"

"I could hardly refuse such a gift," Captain Thorpe cut in upon Lord Exmouth, "for I was told a Hell-Cat is also an incredibly loyal creature. To the right person."

Both men gazed at Miriam with the Hell-Cat curled on her lap.

"I've always been fond of cats." Miriam set the animal down on the deck and stood up to shake hands with Lord Exmouth.

Lord Exmouth saluted Miriam with a kiss on each cheek, reminded her of the Royal Navy's commitment to her support, spoke once again of what he called 'the exit strategy', and wished her Godspeed.

CHAPTER FIVE

In the days after the British Fleet quit the Bay of Algiers, commerce and sea trade slowly recovered. A packet ship from France arrived. Along with the usual load of merchants, seamen, adventurers, and riff-raff, were disgorged two Persian gentlemen. One was a dark-eyed young man in the uniform of the Shah's royal guard, the other an immaculately attired and handsome fellow with the air of a dancing master.

By way first of the palace, this pair came to the barracks where Captain Ansari was recovering of his wounds. Atif Mehmood ushered the two Persian gentlemen in to the captain's chamber.

"Allow me to make myself known, Captain," said the dandier of the pair. "I am Haris Reza, Esquire, of Tehran. My companion is Farrokh Albuyeh Kodio, Cadet in Shah Khaqan's Royal Guard."

Here Haris Reza paused and the gentlemen bowed and greeted one another in the way of their people.

"My uncle Saud Kodio, that is to say, cousin," young Farrokh began, "was kind enough to see us briefly at the palace. We've come to Algiers seeking my sister, Captain, Miriam Albuyeh Kodio."

"My affianced." Haris Reza piped up. Seeing no reaction on the face of the military man, he continued, "My beautiful, my charming Miriam, I only wish to be the dirt upon her threshold, and she has—"

"Right," Farrokh cut in, "she's gone missing, sir, the long and the short of it. My cousin Kodio said he had heard of a young nursemaid using the name of Albuyeh, who came to the villa of the British diplomat about the time of the bombardment."

Captain Ansari regarded the two coolly. The Captain's face reflected nothing of his inward musings, as he compared the remarkable young woman who had slipped into their midst and betrayed them all to the young sprigs before him.

"With two such protectors as yourselves however could Miss Albuyeh have gone missing, is the question I'm asking myself, gentlemen." Captain Ansari hadn't come straight from the womb, the way these youngsters seemed to have done.

Both the young men flushed. Farrokh, with a rapid glance at his companion, hastened to say, "We travelled a long way, sir, from Iran to France. Hearing of her there, that she was engaged as governess to a high born family, recently departed for Algiers, we pursued her...that is, we've come here seeking her. Merely to bring her home to the bosom of her family."

"A bosom, by all appearances, she's rejected?" Captain Ansari glared down his hawkish nose at them.

"Not true," Haris Reza declared, shaking a fine curl out of his eye. "If Miriam does not see the wisdom of her mother and her protectors'—as you name us—choices for her, I'm sure she will soon come to it. Once we have her back, she will become 'a pious spouse fond of obedience and devotion.'"

The young upstart was not the only one who could quote the poets. Captain Ansari replied, "'From a vixen wife protect us well, Save us, O God! from the pains of hell.'"

Taking umbrage, Haris Reza jumped to his feet. "It is obvious you know nothing of Miss Kodio, and would not help us if you did. 'When my raw morsel was cooked and done, Hot from my mouth you took it, and it was gone.'"

Farrokh rose also, his good breeding evident in the way he shook his head in mingled horror and humiliation.

Captain Ansari remained seated. "Forgive me for not seeing you out." The Captain waved a careless hand at his mid-section, where the bandaging was visible through his linen tunic. "Cadet Kodio, might I beg a word with you. One soldier to another."

From his chair, Captain Ansari exchanged a cold bow with Haris Reza, who turned with a harrumph and left the chamber.

"It is all very well to quote the poets," Captain Ansari said, as soon as Farrokh took his seat again, "but you and I are practical men. Are we not? And what man—or woman—of sense can want with that, that—"

"Prancer?" Farrokh suggested.

"Just so."

"It is our mother, mine and Miriam's, who wants Haris, to tell truth. There was a whiff of scandal you see, the merest puff and completely unfounded, linking Miriam and our step-father. Mother wants Haris close, and she calculates the best solution on all fronts is to marry him to Miriam."

Captain Ansari could not keep disapproval from his face, both at Farrokh revealing so much to a stranger and, oddly, at thought of that spirited young woman—betrayer though she might be—tied to such a Prancer.

"A mother's wishes should be honored," Captain Ansari conceded, while thinking there was no wickedness like that of women.

Outside the barracks Haris Reza caught up to Farrokh, took his arm, and smiled into his face.

"Why are you so smug?" Farrokh felt sore, as though he'd been weighed, measured, and found wanting.

"Because, Brother," Haris said, with irritating triumph, "I found out where our little bird has flown."

CHAPTER SIX

52...

Miriam was more comfortable in her new quarters, and with her companions, by the time *Nonesuch* sailed into the true Atlantic. The awkwardness of her first evening alone with Captain Thorpe still troubled Miriam, when she thought back on it.

"Since you have had the great goodness to allow me use of your given name," Captain Thorpe said. "Would you consent to call me Maximus?"

"I would not." Miriam answered at once. Too late she saw hurt, or even loathing, flit across the Captain's features and disappear. "But I shall reserve the right to do so, if I may, at some future time."

She'd risen and curtsied to him then, her heart pounding, and to Miriam's infinite relief Captain Thorpe bowed and smiled. In fact, now they'd been together a score of days, Miriam found Captain Maximus Thorpe a far milder creature than his strange—not to say devilish—appearance might suggest. And it was another queer beast, the Hell-Cat, that allowed Miriam and Captain Thorpe to take the first steps away from being complete strangers.

"What name shall you give it, the Hell-Cat?" Captain Thorpe asked her.

"It is not for me to decide, it was gifted to you," Miriam said. At the same time she put a protective hand on the Hell-Cat, always on her lap whenever she was seated.

Captain Thorpe chuckled. "Oh no, ma'am. Which of us is the beloved is obvious. It may have been given me, but who it chooses to belong to is another matter."

Miriam could not help but be pleased. Besides providing a small common ground between her and her host, she loved a cat as a companion. Having it sleep beside her, watching its carefree capers, promised comfort of a kind Miriam needed in this strange environment. For her time living aboard ship it would be a welcome companion; she had no intention of taking the striking creature with her once the voyage ended.

"That is really very kind in you," she said to Captain Thorpe. "But how shall I name it without knowing if it is female or male?"

"There I can assist you a trifle, by passing along what old Megabazus told me. A Hell-Cat really is an *it*, Miss Miriam, neither he nor she. Though perhaps it would be better to say, they are both he and she. When two Hell-Cats meet, a precious rare thing, they decide which is to...that is to say—" Captain Thorpe blushed and looked away from her.

"Fascinating, though perhaps not unheard of in natural philosophy. I shall just have to think of a name that will do for either." Miriam considered a moment. "I think I have it!"

"Oh aye?" Captain Thorpe cast her a relieved and grateful glance.

"Thrax," Miriam said. "After the ultimate Thracian, which could equally have been man or woman."

Captain Thorpe's mouth was a little agape, and Miriam felt a certain glow of satisfaction. He now knew he was dealing with an educated woman. One thing she could thank Francis Blackwell for was the instruction in Greek and Latin, and mythology she'd had alongside Farrokh. Francis Blackwell had been called progressive and eccentric for allowing a girl the same course of study as a boy.

"Capital, Miss Miriam, well done!" roared Captain Thorpe. In his enthusiasm he leaned toward her, as though he would pat her shoulder.

Thrax seemed to swell and darken in color, whipping round to face Captain Thorpe. For the first time, as it crouched on her lap, Miriam felt its weight and uncoiling power. Captain Thorpe hastily withdrew his hand. Thrax nestled into Miriam's lap again, curling its tail tight against its nose while keeping one eye open and trained on the Captain.

Captain Thorpe let out an uncomfortable laugh. "Well, well, what did I tell you? A Hell-Cat is a loyal creature, one who knows where your best interests lie."

Odd Captain Thorpe certainly was, but Miriam had recovered of her first repugnance to his appearance. From the glimpses she's had of his private life thus far, Miriam was beginning to suspect there were unplumbed depths to Captain Maximus Thorpe. He was no stranger than the rest of his disfigured crew, nor than the ship herself, where odd was concerned.

There was a scratching sound at the great cabin door and the captain's steward Saramago slid into the cabin. He came up to Miriam and offered her a hat of fine fluffy wool.

"For you, Miss," Saramago said. "With my best—how you say?—gallantries."

"How kind, I am very much obliged to you." Miriam turned the closely knitted cap over in her hands. Not many days since Saramago had come in and measured Miriam's head with lengths of package twine. "It is a fine hat, and I am most grateful—"

"From alpaca, Miss, he is a llama gives warmest, best wool."

"I shall be honored to wear it, thank you. I wonder, is it to be so very cold where we are bound?"

Saramago responded with a grin and an enigmatic waggle of his finger back and forth before his own face. A loud and insistent knocking startled the Hell-Cat. Thrax jumped from Miriam's lap with a hiss in the direction of the great cabin door.

"Come in," Miriam called.

Mr. Dashwood rushed in. Miriam was of two minds regarding Mr. Dashwood. Her first evening aboard he'd made her a gift of two bottles of Otto of Roses, that she recognized from when she purchased them in Algiers.

"Where is the Captain?"

Mr. Dashwood was dancing on his toes with excitement.

Miriam motioned toward the right or starboard side of the great cabin, which was Captain Thorpe's exclusive domain. At that moment, hearing Mr. Dashwood's voice no doubt, Maximus Thorpe issued from his private lair. Behind the captain's back, and before he closed the door, Miriam and Mr. Dashwood were treated to a glimpse of luxurious hangings and purpose built wood cabinetry crammed with books and maps. Those rich colored fabrics brought the harem to Miriam's mind, another subject about which she was of two minds, maybe more.

"Well, Mr. Dashwood?"

"We are forty sea miles or so from the gale, sir. And shall close to within twenty in the next glass."

"Very good!" Captain Thorpe clapped his hands loudly. "Saramago! There you are. A pot of tea, Saramago, and pass the word for Mr. Dodd. Mr. Dashwood, we shall clear for action in half a glass. You and Miss Miriam will join me for tea?"

Miriam and Mr. Dashwood looked at one another in confusion.

"Top gallants struck?" Captain Thorpe barked out.

"Why yes, Sir," Mr. Dashwood said, "during this last watch. It may be my first ascent—"

"Just so, Mr. Dashwood," Captain Thorpe said, "and as you've become quite the proficient with the Mechanism, you will be knowing we do have time for tea. This is not just any tea." Captain Thorpe turned to Miriam. "This is *maté*, coca tea, Miss, from Saramago's own country el Perú."

Saramago returned bearing a tray with the tea in cans, each with its pipette. Mr. Dodd followed Saramago in, and they stood thus cramped together, leaving a seasoned old quartermaster at the helm. One by one, once the Captain helped himself, they each—saving Miriam, who went next after Maximum—by rank, selected a can. Then they stood about calmly sipping the *maté*.

"Do be seated, Miss Miriam," Captain Thorpe said. "In a short while we shall make a clean sweep fore and aft. We take down the bulkheads, and remove the furnishings, so that my officers and I have unimpeded passage from one end of the ship to the other."

"From clew to earring, sir," Mr. Dodd offered.

Captain Thorpe smiled, and the bear-like Mr. Dodd rumbled out a chuckle. Mr. Dashwood continued to wear a puzzled expression.

"Mr. Dashwood will be wondering why we take tea before clearing for action," Captain Thorpe said, as though instructing Miriam. "The Incas found that drinking coca tea helped them endure the rarified air of the high Andean mountains, and gave them uncommon resistance to fatigue." The Captain jumped to his feet, having finished his own tea. "Right. Let us shift our clothing, gentlemen, then it's sharps the word and quick's the action. Oh! I was forgetting. Dashwood, have you a pair of trowsers you can give Miss Miriam? You've a narrow backside and they might just fit the lass."

Both Miriam and Mr. Dashwood recoiled as though before a horrid and unthinkable suggestion. Captain Thorpe, already in tearing high spirits, laughed at them. "What a pair of ninnies you are. You are to put on your warmest clothes, Miss, wear the trowsers beneath your skirts if you wish. There is nothing nefarious in it." Captain Thorpe tutted, and said to his first lieutenant, "After you fetch the garment, we shall beat to quarters, Mr. Dashwood."

When Miriam emerged from the closet where she slept, clad in layers of clothing, and fastening a *hijab* over her hair, she met a shipboard world in chaos. The bulkhead partitions, the interior walls, were down and she could see straight through to the bow of the ship. Forward the canvas curtain was removed, so that Captain Thorpe's command center was in plain view. The Captain was standing at the yoke, with Mr. Dashwood practically riding astride the table housing the Mechanism. The carpenter's mates appeared with mallets, and began knocking down the walls of her private den.

Miriam side stepped out of the path of seamen carrying the Captain's personal effects to the hold below the lowest deck of the ship. One of the scurrying men, the bearer of a cabinet box of books, with a pair of candlesticks and plush red velvet curtains atop for good measure, was her China instructor, Jugma Bora. Seaman Bora gave her a distracted shake of the head. The entire deck was opening up to such a degree, Miriam wondered where she must go to keep out of the way.

"Aft there!" Captain Thorpe called out. "Pick up the pace. Ascent in," a pause while Captain Thorpe and Mr. Dashwood exchanged a nod, "one quarter glass. A quarter glass and closing."

The men around her went into a faster whirl of activity. Miriam never expected to see such limping, damaged beings move so fast. They disappeared below decks with their burdens, then came scrambling back up. Some remained on the deck forward of where Miriam crouched on the stern locker in what used to be the great cabin, taking up stations alongside the arrangement of blocks and heavy lines attached to the yoke. Others ran topside where Miriam heard them greeted by

Mr. Dodd. "Mind the lifelines fore and aft!" The motion of the ship had grown lively. It was all Miriam could do to keep her seat.

Saramago came rushing at her at the same time as Captain Thorpe. Mr. Dashwood was holding the yoke now, his long hair streaming behind him.

"Sit down upon the deck itself, Miss Miriam," Captain Thorpe was telling her, kneeling beside her on one knee.

Miriam slid off her seat and did as she was bid, her legs straight out before her, and her back to the stern locker. Several things struck her at once. How glad she was of the trowsers she wore in her present awkward position, and how kind in Captain Thorpe to have thought about her comfort. In fact she was now seated all the way aft and in the starboard area of the ship where *Nonesuch's* captain had his private abode. They were lashing her with lines made fast to the pegs for the cabinets that housed Captain Thorpe's prodigious store of books.

"You shall be able to get free, Miss Miriam, but this will prevent you being too much tossed about, I hope and trust. Saramago! Remember to swallow, Miss." With this strange admonition Captain Thorpe took off forward, stooped over, crab walking sideways with the ship's bucking motion, until he reached the yoke and took over from Mr. Dashwood.

Saramago was still kneeling beside Miriam, alternately sliding into or away from her. From a pocket of his seaman's tunic he withdrew the knitted alpaca hat he'd given her, with its leather reinforced sides meant to cover and protect the ears.

"You forget this in your cabin, Miss," Saramago said. "Wear over your veil, tie under your chin, and pray to Allah to keep us safe. Your ears pain you, chew on this."

The steward pressed into Miriam's palm a small round ball of damp green stuff.

"Coca leaves," he said, "small boiled in lemon water."

Saramago patted her atop her cushioned head, smiled kindly into her face, and was up and away to his appointed station. Under normal circumstances Miriam might resent the steward taking liberties, assuming he knew what god she prayed to, but these were not normal circumstances.

She was so violently tossed from side to side that Miriam popped the coca leaves into her mouth and clung to the ropes binding her. The ship must be nearing the gale the officers spoke of, predicted by the Mechanism. Miriam hung on to the ropes, bruising and chaffing against them, her feet flying in the air. She heard shouting forward, between Captain Thorpe and Mr. Dashwood.

"Course southeast by east, a half east!"

"Mr. Dodd, stunsails a-low. Stuns'ls, Mr. Dodd!"

Mr. Dashwood left the cockpit and ran aft toward Miriam, bent beneath the deck over his head. He did not spare her a glance as he grasped the rails of the aftermost hatchway companion ladder and, stopping halfway up, began shouting orders from Captain Thorpe to the upper deck. The side to side battering ceased, and Miriam felt her stomach rising to her throat. There was a great bump, and a sensation as though the ship was gathered into a giant's hand and then dropped. Miriam's gorge rose up several more times, her ears pained her, and then she remembered to swallow.

Miriam was grateful the flinging about was over. She became aware of a high whistling sound as of a tremendous wind. The cold that set in was sudden and penetrating. She watched her breath cloud in the air before her face. Miriam blessed Saramago and his knit cap. She pulled the lower folds of her *hijab* up over her nose and mouth.

"Mr. Dashwood, set the flotation!" Captain Thorpe called. From his position at the yoke, Captain Thorpe glanced back as his premier dashed up the ladder. "Mr. Dashwood, coat, hat, gloves! Damn your eyes!"

In the moment before Captain Thorpe whipped round to face forward, he met Miriam's gaze. He gave her the briefest of nods, and she caught a regretful look in those eerie mismatched eyes.

Much seemed to be happening on the deck open to the air over her head. Miriam heard shouts and calls, and the stamping of many feet. Captain Thorpe glanced twice more anxiously over his shoulder at the companion ladder.

"Mr. Dashwood!" the Captain thundered. "Report!"

Mr. Dashwood did appear on the companion ladder then, borne slumped between two seamen.

"Stow him in the stern," Captain Thorpe called in a resigned tone, after taking in the situation.

Mr. Dodd came a few steps down the ladder. "Fore and aft flotation in place, Sir! Ready on your word."

The seamen finished securing Mr. Dashwood next to Miriam, and hurried after Mr. Dodd back up the companion ladder. Mr. Dashwood was limp, draped over the lines holding him fast. The ends of his long hair were tipped with frost, and there was a trickle of blood coming from the ear turned toward her. Miriam reached out a trembling hand and put two fingers against Mr. Dashwood's neck. She was relieved to find a strong pulse beating there. More blood was running out one nostril of Mr. Dashwood's sculpted nose.

Unwinding one of Lady Elgin's elegant scarves from round her own neck, Miriam wiped Mr. Dashwood's nose. Then she wrapped the scarf tightly round his head, nose and mouth, the way she'd done her own. Easing out from under the lines restraining her, Miriam made her unsteady way to a rack on the bulkhead in which she'd spotted several boat cloaks.

After tucking a cloak round Mr. Dashwood, inside of the lines, Miriam stumbled forward like a drunkard toward the Captain. Along the way, as she staggered from side to side, she felt guiding and gentle hands placed under her elbow or briefly grip her arm. Miriam found she didn't care when once or twice it was a seaman's metal hook or appendage that grazed her, it made no difference to the assistance afforded her or the kindness with which it was offered.

She made it to the cockpit, and held on to the table surrounding the Mechanism, swinging this way and that, flashing first the brilliant disc with the planets, then one with a compass, and another with astronomical symbols.

Captain Thorpe gave Miriam an inscrutable sideways glance. "How fares Mr. Dashwood? I should almost wish to faint, to be receiving of such tender care."

Miriam was not sure if she'd heard that last part right. "Has he merely fainted? Do you carry a surgeon?"

They were obliged to shout at one another, over the roar of the wind.

"We do not. No extra weight," the Captain said. "We carry our sick and wounded to port. As to Mr. Dashwood, like as not it was the altitude and the rarified air made him take a tumble. Too much enthusiasm by half. Miss Miriam, step this way if you please."

She went to Captain Thorpe, and he moved aside and fixed her hands on the yoke.

"Just for a moment, mind," he said. "Do you see this cross I've drawn on the yoke, and the compass there? The cross is us, Miss Miriam, the *Nonesuch*. Keep her lined up with the compass setting as she is, very well thus."

Her heart began to pound as she felt the live ship humming through the hull, rigging, and the yoke. Captain Thorpe stepped quickly over to the Mechanism and began to adjust it, twirling the various discs around the axis.

"It is a shame and a pity, though who is born to be hanged will never be drowned," Captain Thorpe said, as though to himself. "Mr. Dashwood is a skilled navigator."

The helm was under her control. This was something Miriam, for all her study and love of ships, never dreamed of achieving. She was both thrilled and terrified, fearing the failure of her strength to maintain the course, and anxious every moment for what the next might bring.

Captain Thorpe was back at her side, and taking over the yoke. Her heart raced as she peeled her grip from the helm with reluctance and relief. There was such a connection with the yoke in her hands to the living ship under her control, and of the multitude of forces buffeting *Nonesuch*, that Miriam didn't want the experience to end.

"What do you require, Captain Thorpe?" Miriam shouted. "I can relay orders to the upper deck, I believe."

Miriam remembered a Scottish clansman she'd once seen in Tehran, arrayed in kilt and cloak and weapons, with the same fierce and proud expression Captain Thorpe now turned on her.

"Over there in the bulkhead rack, Miss Miriam, is a speaking trumpet. I would be much obliged to you if you would call up to Mr. Dodd to light the braziers and begin inflation. Once we have her at altitude it will be easier sailing. Use the fore hatchway companion ladder, Miss, the one the men use."

Miriam was positioned halfway up the fore hatchway companion ladder relaying orders between Captain Thorpe and Mr. Dodd. She removed the alpaca hat the better to hear. As Captain Thorpe promised, after a series of commands like, "set the fore staysail, Mr. Dodd. Up rudder and fix wind-engine," the ship's motion became easier, as though in calmer waters.

"Desire Mr. Dodd to take the yoke, if you please, Miss Miriam," Captain Thorpe called.

Mr. Dodd came puffing down, red faced beneath his cap and muffler. Miriam backed down the ladder out of his path. She put the Peruvian cap on again. It was cold and frosty in the ship.

"That was well done, Miss Miriam, very well indeed," Captain Thorpe said. "I beg your pardon for desiring you to stand upon the ladder the hands use, but it is closest to me."

Miriam was surprised by the pleasure those words gave her. "Not at all, Captain."

"Should you like to come on deck with me now?"

Miriam cast a meaning glance in Mr. Dashwood's direction, where the lieutenant was like a cloth doll hung over the ropes.

"Oh, he will keep for the moment, Ma'am," Captain Thorpe said. "You have done a signal service, and ought to see where your efforts have taken us."

Maximus told himself he would not be disappointed if there was shrieking and fainting when he brought Miss Miriam Blackwell up on deck, but the truth was he'd already come to expect better of her. Once Maximus had her secured with a line round her middle to the starboard lifeline, Miriam gazed up at the immense fifty-foot balloons towering over them and asked an intelligent question.

"Montgolfier or Charles, Sir?"

He'd thought her a rare plucked 'un for her behavior earlier, but in that moment Maximus admired her even more.

"They are on the principle of Montgolfier, which is to say hot air balloons," Maximus said. "But with many of the innovations of Charles, the balloons are of silk conditioned in rubber and enclosed in the tremendous nets you see. The whole assemblage requires a deal of maintenance and oversight."

Maximus stopped speaking, catching something familiar in Miriam's dark eyes, a look at once disturbed and thrilled. The rest of her face was hidden by her head scarf. She wore the Peruvian *chuyo*, tied securely beneath her chin, and a boat cloak over all her clothing. He'd made certain she was properly bundled and clothed for the upper deck. One of the greatest sins, to Maximus's mind, was the willing destruction of innocence and beauty.

"The immensity of it, Captain, the silence."

"By Allah, and all the saints of Christendom."

"Amen, amen," Miriam said.

After a decent pause, Maximus turned to her. "Allow me to show you the voltaic pile, that runs the bellows for the great braziers. The braziers are not unlike try pots, ma'am, that are used in our..."

Miriam was swaying on her feet, her knees become wobbly.

"Hand firmly on the line, Miss," Maximus said in a steady voice. "You may put the other on my arm, if you wish."

Miriam stood gripping Maximus and the lifeline, while he faced her with one hand on the line as well. Maximus imagined what she was feeling, for all aboard felt it. The tingling in the feet, that rose up one's body, when you looked out on the immensity of the sky, with clouds below and around you. No land in sight, no sea. You felt as though you could fall headlong into the abyss, and many had.

She took several shuddering breaths. "You will forgive me, I hope, if I cannot move just at present? I should very much like to see your voltaic pile, but I find I...Perhaps you will tell me more about the *Nonesuch*. How...how long shall we sail in the ether?"

"Why, for as long as the wind serves. Deep breaths now, Miss. The wind-engine provides thrust and we steer her with the headsails, do you see? The rudder is no good to us here, in course, and we half ship it and use it as a wind-engine mount."

Miriam nodded with a quizzical expression. Rudder and headsails she may have heard of, but the wind-engine was almost as unknown as the existence of the crack ship herself.

"Those clouds," she said, "I've never seen such beauty, like a blanket of sea foam."

"*Stratus*, they are called, Miss Miriam. I have a transcription of *On the Modification of Clouds*, that classifies them, if you care to read it."

She gazed up into his face, her eyes bright. "She is incomparable, your ship. Truly *Nonesuch* like her."

Her words made Maximus's heart glow. Miriam seemed steadier on her feet now, her grip on his arm lessened. He was grateful she allowed her hand to remain there. Maximus was thinking how best to acknowledge her fine compliment, when a voice broke in on them.

"'The calm Philosopher in ether sails, Views broader stars and breathes purer gales, Sees like a map in many a waving line, Round earth's blue plains her lucid waters shine; Sees at his feet the forky lightning glow, And hears the innocuous thunder roar below.'"

"You have recovered yourself I see, Mr. Dashwood." Maximus turned toward the mooing sound of the lieutenant's voice. "Step this way, if you please."

Miriam's hand dropped from his arm, she held to the lifeline and a stanchion instead.

Mr. Dashwood was at last properly clothed, with a cap over his flowing locks and woolen scarf wrapped round his face. Maximus took his pulse, gripped the lieutenant's head with the fingers of one gloved hand, and peered into his eyes.

"My foster father was an Edinburgh physician, ma'am. Among other things. You asked whether *Nonesuch* had a surgeon. Aboard this ship, we all must do double duty, as we can. I studied Physic and was meant for the medical profession, before I became—"

"An aeronaut!" Mr. Dashwood flung out both arms in an ecstatic way, nearly smacking his captain in the face.

"Steady on, Mr. Dashwood. One hand for the ship. I was meaning to say, mariner."

The ship gave several bumping lurches, and they all three staggered where they stood. Maximus glanced upwards at the balloons, letting his gaze travel down along their net wrappings and the lines securing them to the ship, and then to the braziers and bellows.

"I believe I must ask you to step below, Miss Miriam," he said.

To Maximus's great regret he was not the one to catch her, as Miriam slowly sank to the deck, and then to carry her below. Mr. Dashwood was the more fortunate, and standing closest as Miriam went into a swoon.

CHAPTER SEVEN

Miriam awoke in her tiny sleeping quarters and recollected with a pang what had occurred. She was ashamed and a little incredulous she should have fainted, like the girl who, when the much longed for horseback ride finally comes, falls off and knocks herself senseless. At once she put her hand up and felt a nose and ears that were still whole, with no blood caked to her skin. Maybe it had not been so bad, and she might hope she wasn't entirely disgraced by the episode. Her breath clouded in the air before her, and with the easy motion of the ship, Miriam knew they were still aloft. Still sailing in ether, as Mr. Dashwood had recited from the poem by Erasmus Darwin. Was it the romantic Mr. Dashwood or Captain Thorpe who'd borne her below, and tucked her into her cot?

Someone had left a dark lantern hanging in Miriam's sleeping cabin, with the shutter almost closed, so that she should not be disoriented on waking. A fine, soft, warm woolen blanket covered her. She sighed and pulled the patterned blanket over her nose, stretching and luxuriating. With an inward start Miriam realized who placed it there in her sleeping space, remarkable before for its complete lack of niceties and appointments. Captain Thorpe was its owner and had laid the tartan over her as she lay, vulnerable and insensible. It was difficult to work out how she felt about the Captain, or any man, carrying her about and putting her to bed.

Miriam sat up suddenly to put a stop to a dangerous stream of thought that started with poetry and the sensual luxury of a warm blanket, and moved rapidly on to the erotic. It must be the rarified air. Miriam shook her head and jumped off her shelf like cot. She was wearing Mr. Dashwood's trowsers still, and a tunic with no overdress. She put on a gown hanging from a peg in the cabin, donned *hijab* and cap and great coat, and made a dash for the quarter gallery, the privy in the stern of the ship.

Her timing was good. When she emerged, the seamen with mallets were knocking down bulkhead partitions. Saramago was carrying away an armful of Miriam's bedding, including the fine tartan cloth.

Captain Thorpe came down the after hatchway companion ladder with a great noise of boots on wood, strode up to Miriam, and taking her wrist in one hand, began to take her pulse. He peered into her eyes; it was disconcerting to gaze directly back into those odd colored ones; and pronounced that *she should do.*

"I am glad to hear it, Captain," Miriam said. "And I do beg your pardon for behaving like such a ninny."

That brought an unexpected smile to Captain Thorpe's weary face. He made a secretive gesture toward Mr. Dashwood, coming up behind them, and murmured, "I wish all parties aboard had your good sense, Miss."

"I am obliged for your kind care of me. And grateful I didn't take frost bite." She realized now what ailed some of the crew, and that it was their captain who tended them.

"God between us and evil."

Saramago came in and served the three of them cans of *maté*, and then went forward to bring Mr. Dodd his tot. Looking at the two tired faces as they sipped, Miriam recalled the Captain's words about the care and attention that must be paid to their canopy, the balloons that kept them in the air. She supposed the officers, Captain Thorpe and Mr. Dashwood and

Mr. Dodd, and many of the seamen, were on duty during the entirety of *Nonesuch's* time aloft. How long exactly that had been, Miriam was unsure.

She felt a gut level need to understand how the ship worked, and how they were to make the descent. Wasn't that why they were once again drinking *maté*? A little knowledge would go a long way toward balancing her terror at sailing in *Nonesuch* with her wonder.

Miriam decided to brazen it out, risk overstepping a boundary by questioning the ship's captain. "Is there a reason we are to come down just here, Captain Thorpe, and in the nighttime?"

Much to her relief, Captain Thorpe set his empty can down on the tray, and turned to her with an enlivened and eager countenance.

"A capital question, Miss Miriam, and very observant in you to discover we mean to descend. Mr. Dashwood's reading of the Mechanism puts us several hundred leagues from the Cape, and with the blessing we shall make the prettiest landfall at Table Bay within the week. As to the nighttime, well Miss." Captain Thorpe broke off and grinned at Miriam and Mr. Dashwood in turn. "A sailor will think he's seeing things if he catches sight of a ship descending from the night sky, but during the daylight hours he is not so easy to persuade."

"That's correct, ma'am," Mr. Dashwood said, "crack ships are clandestine, we always descend at night."

Captain Thorpe shook his head at this, and glanced warily at Miriam.

"We need the lift from strong winds to help us ascend, and fine weather and darkness, if we can get it, Ma'am, to smooth our way down. Mr. Dashwood, please to relieve Mr. Dodd at the yoke, and send him to me on deck."

Miriam calculated it must be nearly time for her to be strapped in the stern with ropes, so she spoke at once. "Captain Thorpe, if I may be so bold."

He turned from having been about to hurry off, and bowed to her. Miriam was conscious of his sudden concentrated attention on her.

"You spoke about everyone aboard doing a double duty, and I wanted to offer my...ah, services. If there is any small service I might perform. As during the ascent?"

She immediately regretted her tone, and having put that last as a question. It sounded at once both too forward and over-subservient, neither of which she meant to be. Miriam found Captain Thorpe nodding at her with a kind expression, and she added, "I am determined not to faint again."

He opened his mouth to speak, and closed it again, considering. "Wrap yourself warmly then, Miss, and you may accompany me on deck for the readings. You shall free one of the lieutenants from attending me."

On deck once more, where Miriam found she'd wanted to be since waking from her faint, the terror and grandeur of the night enveloped her. This was what she'd longed to experience again. The wisps of cloud floating by, the overarching night sky like a pierced dome with a multitude of brilliant stars shining through. Closer. They were nearer to the stars here in the ether than she'd ever thought possible. Miriam gazed at it all and recalled those lines in Persian, "my soul it drinks wine, and is wild with delight."

Like Mr. Dashwood, Miriam wanted to share her joy, though she'd thought him rather silly at the time springing up spouting poetry. It brought to mind other canting individuals she'd known. But it was possible she judged too harshly. Miriam wanted to translate the fine Persian sentiment, that so exactly described the feeling of being on the deck of *Nonesuch* in the open night air, and share it with the ship's captain.

Captain Thorpe was attending to business, his head not in the clouds with hers and Mr. Dashwood's. He put a line round Miriam's waist and clapped it to the lifeline in a trice. Captain Thorpe led her past the voltaic pile of six hundred four inch square double plates, explaining as they went their function in powering the bellows that stoked the enormous braziers. The famous pile was what Miriam had mistaken for the ship's boats, underneath a canvas covering on the deck. She stood behind Captain Thorpe as he paused to order the men attending the braziers to begin reducing fuel.

He moved toward the front of the ship and once past the braziers and the shadow of the great balloons, the view on deck opened up. Miriam's head spun with the immensity of the vista. The endless space and glorious stars above, and looking over the ship's side, through wispy clouds, Miriam caught sight of lapping waves and the sea. She fervently hoped she was not to faint again, she felt a tingling in her feet that was rising to fill her whole person.

"Captain Thorpe!"

The Captain glanced back at Miriam over his shoulder. He had one hand on the lifeline, while tucked beneath the other arm was one of the ship's journals and his instruments.

"You may take hold of my arm, or my coat, Miss. In a few paces we shall halt and you can sit upon the deck, to make note of the readings. Will that suit you?"

Miriam nodded, struck dumb, chewing hard on the plug of coca leaves Saramago had given her earlier. She took a seat on the deck in a spot indicated by the Captain. Miriam felt it would be all she could manage to write a legible hand, through her layers of gloves and with her trembling fingers.

Try she must though, for Captain Thorpe was actually letting go the lifeline in order to take proper hold first of sextant, and then barometer and theodolite. Miriam dipped her quill pen and waited as he stood feet apart, taking a celestial sighting and then atmospheric pressure and temperature.

Captain Thorpe called the readings to her in a strong voice, and Miriam did her best to scratch them carefully in the places he'd shown her in the journal. Bless the man, Miriam thought when she finished the inscriptions and looked up at Captain Thorpe with the dark heavens framing him, for allowing her a small part in this wonder.

"Do take hold of the line, Captain Thorpe, I beg."

He smiled and did as she asked. Captain Thorpe went down on one knee beside her and examined her notations.

"That's very pretty writ, Miss, I am obliged to you. In a moment we shall proceed below decks, where I must leave you."

Miriam nodded, replacing the pen and ink pot in a pocket of her boat cloak. "I hope I can manage better than to crawl there."

Captain Thorpe gave her a look of affection, if Miriam did not mistake, but he was prevented from making any remark by the appearance of Mr. Dodd. Or, from Miriam's perspective, Mr. Dodd's heavy boots.

"Wind-engine dismounted and ready to cast off ballast, Sir."

"Very good, Mr. Dodd, stand by if you please. I will take Miss Albuyeh below and then I shall be with you, and we will begin the countdown procedure."

Miriam swallowed hard and stood, and faced about on the lifeline from which she'd never been detached. She fought the paralysis that wanted to grip her and forced one foot in front of the other. As she plodded back to the after hatchway companion ladder she kept her head up and tried to fix it all in her mind. The towering balloons overhead, sagging now or beginning to, and the men stationed by the voltaic pile and slowly feeding the braziers. More men were gathered near the main chains on both sides of the ship, ready to cast off ballast at the captain's word. Miriam was aware Captain Thorpe was trusting her with a great deal, allowing her to see so much of his ship and her operations.

Below decks Miriam descended into the relative comfort of the enclosed environment. It was a degree or two warmer, and there were familiar faces. Jugma Bora, his eyes large in his head, was stationed alongside a port side cable running between the yoke and the upper works. Saramago appeared as soon as the captain's foot touched the gun deck, and he relieved Captain Thorpe of the journal, barometer, and other instruments.

"You will allow Saramago and me to lash you in the stern once more, Miss Miriam," Captain Thorpe said, as soon as his steward returned from storing the instruments. "I hope and trust?"

Miriam's heart began to pound as they tied her against the stern lockers. She wished she could take in the whole spectacle from the upper deck, if only she could be quite certain of not face planting into it.

"Spit out the coca leaves, Miss," Captain Thorpe said, startling Miriam. "Spit them right out. Here you are, Saramago has a basin."

She removed the quid delicately from her mouth with two fingers and placed it in the pewter cup Saramago extended, it was not the oddest thing yet to occur. For no particular reason, Miriam said, "I wonder where Thrax has got to?"

"Pissamdeared," Saramago said.

"I believe what he means is, disappeared." Captain Thorpe pulled on the lines binding Miriam in the stern to make sure they were fast. Then he rose, bowed to her, called forward to Mr. Dashwood at the yoke, and hurried up the companion ladder.

A great shouting and stomping broke out on the upper deck. Mr. Dodd appeared on the companion ladder and relayed orders to Mr. Dashwood. Miriam experienced that sensation of her stomach rising and dropping again. Captain Thorpe ran heavily down the fore hatchway companion ladder and took over from Mr. Dashwood at the yoke.

"Aft! Aft, Mr. Dashwood, and let go the hundred weight ballast at the word!"

Captain Thorpe appeared to wrestle the yoke, bearing it down by degrees, shouting orders over his shoulder at Mr. Dashwood.

"Strike stunsails," Captain Thorpe called in a strong voice. "Let go the hundred weights!"

Mr. Dashwood shouted to the upper deck. *Nonesuch's* descent slowed as the ballast was cast off. There came several more sickening falls and recoveries, and then a smacking collision followed by a series of severe bumps as though *Nonesuch* were dragging across a reef.

"Huzzah!" cried Mr. Dashwood.

In his exuberance and joy Mr. Dashwood lost his grip, and as the vessel careened along he was thrown backward off the ladder. He landed on his backside and slid nearly to Miriam in the stern, his long legs curving round to come to rest near hers.

"Now is not the time for tomfoolery, Mr. Dashwood." Captain Thorpe ran aft and gave Mr. Dashwood his hand to help him rise.

Gripping the Captain's hand, Mr. Dashwood swayed into an upright position. "Any landing you sail away from is a good landing, so it is said among aeronauts, Miss Miriam."

Captain Thorpe's brows lowered in a pained expression, as though Mr. Dashwood were giving away a club secret.

"Come, Mr. Dashwood, if you are unhurt," Captain Thorpe said. "The rudder will not ship itself, and there is much to attend to before we will be having ourselves a comfortable caulk."

Captain Thorpe was moving to follow the first lieutenant up the companion ladder when he suddenly whipped round, strode over, and gave his hand to Miriam as she was casting off the lines about her.

"Forgive me for using the sailor's cant before you, and for being a laggard in gentlemanly ways." Captain Thorpe assisted her to her feet. "You've done so well I begin to think of you as a right sailor. The carpenter's mates will be putting up the bulkheads, the walls that is, and you shall have your private space back soon."

Privacy was the last thing Miriam craved at that moment. Captain Thorpe couldn't know how strongly his words had struck her, nor how inspired she felt by the experience of...flight. Now Miriam had named it, she wanted to talk about it, to jump and shout 'Huzzah' like Mr. Dashwood. But of course, she wouldn't detain the Captain.

Miriam thanked Captain Thorpe and curtsied to him.

"Only look, here is Thrax!" Captain Thorpe cried, leaning down to pat the Hell-Cat's head. Thrax evaded his outstretched hand. "The rogue, coming along when all the excitement is done!"

CHAPTER EIGHT

The ascent and descent into the South Atlantic integrated the newcomers almost as thoroughly as a battle would have done, in Maximus Thorpe's estimation. They'd lain to for a day to rest and recover, and were presently under easy sail for the Cape of Good Hope, Africa. Though he might suffer from an excess of zeal, Mr. Dashwood was proving an excellent navigator and a proficient with the Mechanism. In spite of his early swoon, Mr. Dashwood recovered, and he'd not done badly with the management of crew, sails, flotation, and ballast. Overall, Maximus was pleased. Mr. Valentine Dashwood might do very well.

The other recruit foisted on him in Algiers, Maximus was less sure about. He'd not been so taken up during the time aloft that he'd failed to notice Jugma Bora's haunted look, like an animal in the slaughterhouse. Maximus was offended. His ship was the product of a modern age of navigation, not an abattoir where people expected to die.

Maximus turned to his passenger, another first voyager. He now felt Miriam was part of the life of the ship, having shown herself equal to the strange requirements of *Nonesuch*. Miriam Albuyeh Kodio Blackwell sat across from him reading Howard's *On the Modification of Clouds*.

"Shall I send for seaman Bora?" Maximus asked. The language lessons were of course suspended during the last active days. "It is his off watch."

Miriam looked up at him, glanced out the stern windows, and at the chronometer over his head.

"It is the time of sunset prayers, but I should be obliged if you did send for him in another half hour." Miriam set down the *Philosophical Journal* containing the transcription of Howard's lecture. "You recall me to the duty before me, Captain Thorpe. I had best remove my head from the clouds."

Maximus had not at all wished to do so, to hurry his guest toward a dangerous and uncertain future. Guilt flooded in. He knew he was doing just that, it was his assigned duty on this mission. The trouble was, Maximus was finding that he should like to keep Miriam there with him, with her lovely head firmly in the clouds.

"Bora is a Mohammedan, I collect?" Maximus ventured. "As I take it you are too, ma'am, since you know their ways."

By her change of expression, Maximus realized he'd blundered again. Trespassed a personal boundary, as when he'd asked her to call him by his first name.

"Iran is an Islamic country," she said. "As is much of Java and Malaya, Jugma Bora tells me. So it is natural you should think I am Muslim. Do I take it, sir, since you are from a Christian nation, you are also a Christian?"

His simple bow and assent belied a complicated history, and Maximus cursed whatever impulse made him bring it up. He was born to a Roman Catholic family of Scotland, but must declare for the Anglican church and England in order to serve as an officer in the King's Navy.

"You would be surprised at how much Christianity and Islam have in common, perhaps, Captain Thorpe," Miriam said, with a kind smile.

For a moment he had forgot with whom he was dealing. "How is that, Ma'am?"

"They are both monotheistic: There is only one God. Both have certain moral laws or tenants. And within both Christianity and Islam, there exist many divisions or sects."

She was a woman a man could really talk to, and his enthusiasm led Maximus to ask another impertinent question. "How did you come to such knowledge of the world's great religions?"

He was relieved when Miriam smiled.

"Like you, Captain, I enjoy reading." She motioned round at the many books that had made their way from Maximus's private space into her sitting area. "If I have a love of learning, of the getting of knowledge, it is probably due to an English step-father who believed a girl's mind as worthy of developing as a boy's."

Miriam stopped speaking and peered at him in a self-conscious way. Maximus wondered if other women of Persia were half so beautiful and wise.

"Mr. Francis Blackwell, the diplomat," Maximus said, with a nod.

"I was forgetting you will have had my history from Lord Exmouth." Miriam frowned. "I came to maturity in Muslim countries, and was educated by a westerner and a Christian. As to which I cling to I must say neither, since I have put myself beyond the pale of both."

Maximus's throat went dry. That such a lovely, modest, intelligent woman could feel this way shocked him. He hoped he didn't pry too much into her affairs. "How can that be?" he asked.

Her dark eyes took on an inward, weary cast. "I left my home in Iran, and the protection of my mother and brother, and went among foreigners. I go about unveiled, and live in the company of men who are not my brothers, or my father, or husband. Neither Christians nor Muslims countenance such things."

His first instinct was to argue with her, to deny and assert extenuating circumstances. To claim no one would think the worst of a woman unprotected in the world, making her own way among foreigners. But wouldn't they? Maximus knew the answer, the world was a scandal loving unromantic place. He could hardly look into Miriam's face, it was so clouded over with trouble and pain.

"I beg your pardon if I have distressed you with my unseemly curiosity," Maximus said at last. He was deeply sensible of his own part in Miriam's difficulties, and he determined, rather than dwell on his guilt and desires, to try to aid this young person he was growing fonder of daily. "I shall send for seaman Bora now, with your leave. And I should wish to begin another course of study with you, if you are willing. To impart some of the anatomical knowledge I came by in Edinburgh." Maximus didn't add, as he did inwardly, so that she should be able to thrust a knife into the most vulnerable parts of a man—or woman.

Sounds of a commotion on deck reached Miriam, Captain Thorpe, and seaman Bora seated round the table in the great cabin. Clomping steps were heard on the after hatchway companion ladder and after knocking, Mr. Dodd loomed in the great cabin doorway.

"What is it, Mr. Dodd?" Captain Thorpe half rose from his seat.

"Flying fish, sir. Two of the devils became involved with the wind-engine, sir, I am sorry to report."

"Och, no!" Captain Thorpe was on his feet at once. "Improper securing of the wind-engine, Mr. Dodd, this is what comes of it! Miss Miriam, Bora, you may continue the lesson on the gangways and forecastle."

On deck Captain Thorpe turned aft to deal with the fouled engine, while Miriam and Jugma Bora walked forward. As they wove through the seamen pirouetting and leaping with nets to collect the flying fish still coming aboard—everyone knew flying fish ate well indeed—Miriam repeated to Jugma Bora the simple phrases they'd been practicing in the cabin. Together they halted on the quieter forecastle and Miriam fell silent, watching the white foam slide down *Nonesuch's* sides into a purplish sea as the ship parted the waves.

"I know you were raised in the harem," Bora said of a sudden, in Malay.

Miriam opened her mouth to protest such familiarity, but Jugma Bora interposed.

"Very well, you understand me. Save your blame, I will hear it when you answer in the same tongue."

With a swift glance toward the quarterdeck where Captain Thorpe was bent over the wind-engine, Miriam nodded and turned her gaze again on the bow wave thrown hypnotically up and up.

"Your conduct announces it," Jugma Bora continued in his native Siamese, "to all but the clueless foreigner." He jerked his head toward the knot of officers and seamen surrounding Captain Thorpe. "The way you read men and your surroundings, as though your life depended on it. Maybe it did?"

"No," Miriam said in the language of Siam. "You know nothing."

"Good on you, Miss." A satisfied smirk crossed Bora's face. "Now, open your ears and learn. I know a woman like you, raised to lead a circumscribed life. Even more so in my honored aunty's case, the fashion of the day imposing physical subservience on her body."

Jugma Bora paused and Miriam shivered, imagining what this could mean. Night closed round them. Phosphorescent points of light began to appear in the sea surrounding the ship, like twinkling reflections of the first stars in the heavens above.

"She was meant to be a silent decoration to some rich man's household but this aunty married well, to a man with many ships. He built an empire from those ships and the rich cargos of the South China Sea. And then her husband died."

Mesmerized by the never ending bow wave, and the sparkling surface of the sea, Miriam concentrated on Jugma Bora's last words, spoken in Mandarin. She searched her mind and found understanding and ability.

"What became of honored ancestor?" she said.

"No, not ancestor for she lives yet." Jugma Bora shook his head, speaking Malay. "Honored Aunty took control of the fleet of ships, three hundred and more. This woman, shrewd and fearless though raised to modesty and obedience, increased the plunder of her husband's house a thousand fold. Think of it, Miss, what it would mean to such a woman to be the commander, instead of the commanded!"

Miriam turned her gaze from the brilliant multifaceted light of sea and sky and for the first time met Jugma Bora's eyes. The eager expectancy on his face startled Miriam, she felt pulled from a trance and struggled to remember the language they'd been speaking and the import of the words.

As though to prompt her, Bora said, "What would it mean to you, Miss, to command such a ship as this one? Were you to bring this ship a prize to my honored aunty, she might make you her heir."

A shadow moved out of the darkness behind Jugma Bora's left shoulder. All was quiet on deck, the smells of frying flying fish drifted from the galley stove. Miriam watched Captain Thorpe approaching to join them, she wondered how long he'd been there listening, hidden by the gloom.

Miriam leaned toward Jugma Bora, and very low in Malay, she said, "What it would mean is mutiny, and I beg you will speak no more about it."

Captain Thorpe pointed out to Miriam the Table Mountain with a ring of cloud suspended half way down its slopes, which also formed a mane and ruff round the dome shaped Lion's Head. Lion's Rump, Devil's Hill, and a vast range of mountains lay beyond. Before the Cape was raised Miriam hadn't spent much time on the upper deck. She'd been obliged to keep out of the way of the swaying up of the guns, and the stowage down into the hold of the great balloons. Captain Thorpe and Mr. Dashwood were so taken up in their labors that Miriam hardly exchanged a word with either one. She sensed a certain hesitation, an unnatural formality in his manner, as Captain Thorpe named the Table Bay landmarks to her.

Miriam wasn't rid of the uncomfortable feelings left by their last serious conversation and what he might have overheard of her lesson with Jugma Bora. Why she'd spoken so openly before to Captain Thorpe, of faith and other private matters, she didn't know. The afterglow of exhilarating flight might account for part of it. It couldn't be the reason she'd accepted his offer of instruction in "anatomy". Miriam would have to be much thicker-headed than she was not to realize Captain Thorpe was teaching her self-defense—to fight. She'd gone about violating every tenant of silence, of modesty, of keeping herself to herself, that had ruled her life to this point. Miriam couldn't be easy on that score, Jugma Bora's legends of fabulous women notwithstanding.

"*Jupiter* is making our number, sir," Mr. Dodd reported.

"So I see, Mr. Dodd, I thank you."

Captain Thorpe turned to Miriam, and made a stiff bow. "The next signal will be 'captain repair aboard', ma'am, so I must take leave of you."

Captain Losack, HMS *Jupiter*, the senior officer on the Cape of Good Hope station, was known in the Service for two things; an eccentric wife who accompanied him in his sea-going commands, and the keeping of an excellent table. Upon his entrance in *Jupiter*'s cabin, the captain's lady accosted Maximus with the declaration she'd seen a woman on the deck of *Nonesuch*. She thrust a glass of Château Lafite into his hand, and demanded the particulars.

"Why, ma'am, that is Miss Miriam Blackwell. She is my guest for the Eastward passage. She is to be met by her father, a gentleman in the diplomatic service."

"Is she an Oriental?" Lady Losack, as she was known to the crew of HMS *Jupiter*, turned to her husband. "One can always tell by the head-scarf. A veil or a turban are sure signs of your Mohammedan."

Maximus's face flushed. "Miss Blackwell is a Persian lady, ma'am. As to her faith, we are not well enough acquainted that I should have discovered that much."

"What a honey'd way of speaking you Scotsmen have, Maximus. Any lady would be proud to have such a champion." Lady Losack all but winked at him. "May I call you Maximus? Such a strong name, it brings to mind the Romans. Were you called after an Emperor or a Caesar, sir?"

"My father was an antiquities scholar, ma'am." Maximus bowed, wondering if he'd been this goddamn forward and impertinent with Miss Miriam.

Hours later Maximum went down the side of *Jupiter* into his own boat, well lubricated with superior wine and vittles. In his pocket was a letter of invitation that Maximus believed, in the muzzy headed glow of the moment, could not but bring pleasure to his lady guest.

Next day Miriam and Mr. Dashwood stood together on *Nonesuch's* larboard gangway, watching the captain's gig approach. Miriam was to be rowed ashore to meet Captain Thorpe in Cape Town for the start of their excursion. Beyond the village of Cape Town, growing sunshine lifted the clouds draped like a damask shawl round the shoulders of Table Mountain.

"I know this outing can hardly please a retiring lady like you, Miss Miriam," Mr. Dashwood said, shaking back his long hair as it stirred in the gentle breeze.

The invitation to dine at the home of a Dutch landholder where the British governor's lady hostess was holding court didn't please Miriam, but she would be sorry if that much was evident to Mr. Dashwood.

"There is no help for it, I am afraid, Mr. Dashwood. I was spotted on deck, Captain Thorpe informs me. Resistance is futile." Or worse would call more unwanted attention to her. Miriam tried for a cheerful tone. "I would have to confine myself below decks to avoid notice, a thing I'm most unwilling to do. For what is life without sunlight and fresh air?"

Miriam expected the enthusiastic lieutenant to agree with her. Instead, as though she hadn't spoken at all, Mr. Dashwood said, "It is want of sensibility on the Captain's part, that he cannot see you prefer to remain anonymous to the shore. If you wish I will meet Captain Thorpe on the quay and make your excuses, I would be perfectly happy to do so."

Miriam suppressed the first sharp retort that rose to her lips.

Mr. Dashwood mistook her hesitancy for delicacy of manner and indecision. "He was advised to hire an ox-cart for the drive to Groot Constantia, instead he has gone ahead to scour the town for the best horse and carriage." Mr. Dashwood sniffed. "I will say nothing of a certain national tendency for showing away."

Miriam took a deep breath. "I'm very much obliged to you, Mr. Dashwood, but it is a glorious day and I must say I'm rather looking forward to seeing something of Africa."

The eighteen or twenty picturesque farms, as though transplanted from Holland each with its own flour mill, were left far behind at the bottom of Devil's Hill and Table Mountain. The pony trap driven by Captain Thorpe was wending its way through a hilly, verdant countryside. Jostling along, and having narrowly avoided an ox-cart, Miriam thought it incumbent on her to comment on the conveyance.

"How did you come by your skills, Captain Thorpe?" she asked, clasping her head scarf under her chin with one hand. "You are a capital whip."

Captain Thorpe chuckled, over her use of the latest slang phrase or maybe because it was a day to gladden the heart. High cumulus cloud drifted in a vast, piercingly blue sky overhead.

"One learns a few things at university, ma'am," Captain Thorpe said. "How to drive four in hand, how to fight with sword and pistol. In Edinburgh they are much given to dueling."

"How unfortunate. Or is it not so for you Physical gentlemen? Since you may practice your art by sewing on their ears, and putting them back together."

Captain Thorpe laughed and glanced at her with an appreciative glint in his eye. "I shall slow the horse if you wish."

They were at a walking pace when the road, with grape vines on one hand stretching away across the hills, made a turning and ran beside a long barn, with an adjoining corral or outdoor pen. Miriam noticed guard towers at the outside corners of the complex.

"What is this place?" She shuddered and wished she hadn't asked, for she began to see what it was as they drove slowly past.

Captain Thorpe frowned. "It is a place they keep slaves. A prison for the ones who tried to run away, or committed some other transgression."

Miriam stared through the fencing of the corral area, inside were posts and large wooden triangles stained red with blood. "I thought...is not slavery abolished in Britain, sir?" Her lips felt odd and numb.

"This is not exactly England," Captain Thorpe said, not unkindly. "And I apprehend this place is a private concern, run by the local landholders. Those who own these beautiful vineyards you and I have been admiring."

Whose food and wine they would shortly be eating and drinking; Miriam hoped it might not stick in her throat. They were driving past the extreme end of the corral. Inside of it, a number of women and children were gathered. As the pony trap came level with them, the women pushed their arms through the spaces between the wooden slats and the children cried out with one voice.

Miriam at last turned back round on the bench seat from staring at the heartbreaking little group. Captain Thorpe's face was grave, and she suspected he'd understood their speech. "How can women and children be confined in such a place!" Hesitating, she added, "What did the children say?"

"I wish I had known the track runs this way," he muttered, as though to himself. Captain Thorpe turned to her. "Please, Miss. They said please."

Miriam and Captain Thorpe were seated across from one another, and far down the table from the Governor's hostess, Lady Anne, and her important guests, Captain and Lady Losack. Upon arrival they'd been cordially greeted by this triumvirate, along with a collection of officers of the 31st Highlanders, and a number of civilians. Among the Scottish officers was an army surgeon of Captain Thorpe's acquaintance, Doctor Polidari, who was Miriam's left hand neighbor at table. On her right was a clergyman who was already eyeing her askance, but with whom she would be forced to converse at some point during dinner.

While the first vegetable courses were served Miriam was free to speak to Doctor Polidari, a little, dark, drab and unobtrusive man with a penetrating gaze.

"Oh yes," Doctor Polidari said, in response to Miriam's inquiring whether he and Captain Thorpe were acquainted in Edinburgh. "We go back to University days, and even before. I was a correspondent of Maximus's foster-father. A unique gentleman, ever willing to receive and treat with a foreigner. I knew Maximus when his eyes were the same color."

Miriam was intrigued by this statement, but before she could make any rejoinder, a burly red faced man across the table, a civilian seated next to Captain Thorpe, declared so loudly as to call everyone's attention, "Tell us of the bombardment of Algiers, Captain, I understand your ship was there. A glorious action, a stunning victory, by all accounts. But what else is to be expected in an encounter between good English Tars and mere Turks and Arabs."

The beefy man cast a malignant stare in Miriam and Doctor Polidari's general direction. Miriam was unsure for whom, exactly, it was meant. The Highland officers stirred uneasily, while the witty banter between Lady Anne and Captain and Lady Losack up table was momentarily suspended.

"I regret to disappoint you, sir." Captain Thorpe spoke into the waiting silence. "The ship under my command was not present at the actual battle."

"Quite right, Harriman," Captain Losack called, "*Nonesuch* was ordered in after the excitement, in support of the Fleet."

"Surely the Captain must have heard accounts, from those more fortunate in being upon the scene of glory?" Harriman fired back. "Share one or two anecdotes with us, I beg Captain Thorpe. I hear the Mohammedans were notoriously undisciplined creatures. Nearly as bad as our Hottentots."

Another rapid and furious glance from Harriman seemed to encompass Miriam, Doctor Polidari, and the black man serving them. This time Miriam felt sure she was merely on the periphery of the man's malignancy. Captain Thorpe caught Miriam's eye, and an unhappy concerned look passed between them.

"I..." Captain Thorpe began.

"If it's the view of the Mohammedans you're after," Lady Losack put in, "you may as well ask it of Miss Blackwell. She's Persian."

Heads whipped round and everyone stared at Miriam. She clasped her hands together to keep them still in her lap, and returned Lady Losack's gaze directly, resisting the urge to touch or adjust her *hijab*.

"What do I care from Persia?" Harriman declared. "We were speaking of the conniving, turban wearing—"

"A glass of wine with you, Captain Thorpe," Captain Losack called loudly, with a quelling look at the choleric Harriman. "And a toast! Here is to the brilliant success of the Fleet under the estimable Lord Exmouth!"

After everyone drank the toast, each turned with unspoken accord to address their right hand neighbor. Multiple conversations broke out again.

"The freeing of thousands of Christian slaves," the clergyman on her right said to Miriam, "after the bombardment of Algiers, cannot be viewed as anything but the righting of a great wrong."

A black man leaned between Miriam and the clergyman, proffering a dish of potatoes and onions. Angry red welts round the man's wrist were exposed as he extended the platter.

"Oppression of any people, anywhere, must be a great wrong, sir," Miriam said.

The clergyman sniffed. "I would not go so far as that, madam, for then the discussion becomes a Philosophical one. What constitutes oppression, and what is done for the good of a people. Take our own black tribesmen here in Little

Constantia as an example, a more feckless, ignorant, dirty set of heathens was never to be met with—"

"Hear him!" called Harriman. "We Britons are the first race in the world, and the more of it we inhabit the better for the human race."

"He shall launch next into phrenology," Doctor Polidari muttered. "God give me patience."

"It is a well known fact," Harriman declared, "that the skull of a bushman differs significantly from that of a gentleman."

"For one," Polidari said, low and to no one in particular, "it is not scarred and bruised the way a black man's of this country is like to be."

Doctor Polidari's remark went unnoticed by all but Harriman, who glowered mightily. A large dish of mutton cutlets fried with crumbs of bread and pickles was served, followed by tripes, soup and fish, and a final course of great joints of roast mutton and beef. At last Lady Anne invited her guests to take coffee and fruit on the terrace. In the confusion and clatter as the party rose from table Miriam secreted a number of bread rolls in her reticule, into the center of which she'd stuffed hunks of roast mutton.

Miriam was obliged to take a seat near Lady Anne and Lady Losack, as the only other females of the party, while the gentlemen smoked cigars and strolled the plantation grounds. Lady Anne's little pug dog began to show an eager interest in Miriam.

"Come away, Jules," Lady Anne cooed, pulling the dog off Miriam's knees. "It is an impertinent creature, is it not?" She grasped the dog's head as she spoke to it, even allowing the upturned black muzzle and tongue to wet her cheek.

Miriam and Thrax touched noses, yet such liberties seemed far more repugnant with a dog. Jules, the pug, gave Miriam and her reticule a significant woof, and ran a lolling tongue over an already moist nose and upper lip.

"I beg your pardon for subjecting you to such a dinner, Miss Blackwell," Lady Anne said of a sudden. "You may have remarked Mr. Harriman's, ah, antipathy to Doctor Polidari?"

Lady Anne and Lady Losack exchanged a glance, and it was Lady Losack who took up the tale. "Harriman is a considerable land holder in Little Constantia, and Big Constantia too. Doctor Polidari had the effrontery to offer his services in a medical capacity to those unfortunate inmates of Harriman's Hole. Did you remark the place as you passed this way?"

"I did," Miriam said, holding her reticule tighter.

"Mr. Harriman is a gross man," Lady Anne put in softly, "and received Doctor Polidari's suggestion in the most ill-tempered and froward manner. Mr. Harriman cannot be made to understand if he insults Doctor Polidari, he offends his entire regiment."

"Doctor Polidari is the much esteemed surgeon of the Thirty-First," Lady Losack told Miriam. "An eminent hand with a lancet or scalpel, top of his college at Edinburgh, but he was born in Constantinople."

Miriam tried to keep her many feelings from showing on her face, her instant understanding of the root of all those menacing glares from Harriman at table, and her wonder at the two ladies with whom she sat for bringing these men together.

"Was this dinner an attempt at peace-making?" Miriam said.

"Just so!" Lady Anne cried. "How perceptive you are, Miss Blackwell. But it has gone terribly wrong, I'm afraid."

Ill judged and ill managed was how Miriam would have put it. Why had these women allowed the aggrieved parties to sit near one another, while they held a separate confabulation at their end of the table?

"Some people just do not understand what it is to be oppressed." Lady Losack inclined her head to Miriam. "I suppose you should be very glad to be told you need not go about showing only this much of your face." With her hands, Lady Losack framed her own face as though wearing the veil.

Miriam glanced down, and thought of what Doctor Polidari said earlier. *God give me patience.*

"No, I should not be glad, ma'am," Miriam said, "for no one tells me what I must or must not wear. Do they you?"

Lady Anne snickered. Lady Losack was dressed, as was her custom, in an extraordinary way. She wore a long naval style jacket in blue broadcloth with gold lace, an epaulette on each shoulder, with her gown and petticoats underneath.

Lady Losack reared back, taking hold of her brass buttoned lapels, primed to return fire. But she was cut off by Mr. Harriman stomping up to them on the terrace. He came in company with Captain Losack to take his leave. Miriam rose and retreated, unremarked by any of the important people.

She and Captain Thorpe were among the last to escape. Miriam took the opportunity of bringing up the end of the line to thank their hosts, to cram several oranges left on the coffee tables into the top of her reticule. Eventually they emerged on to the sunlit front porch, facing the track that passed before the plantation house. Most of the Highland officers were mounted up and away, but a few stragglers still awaited their horses. The pony trap Captain Thorpe had engaged was held by a black man at the bottom of the steps.

"I don't give two bloody shits for those wooly headed black bastards, or for you, you misbegotten brown pill-driving bugger!"

This vulgarity was flung out into the tranquil afternoon air by a flushed and furious Harriman. The big beefy man and Doctor Polidari were standing toe to toe in the carriageway. Captain Thorpe ran down the steps toward them, extending his arm out to Miriam as though to hold her off.

"Will you answer for that, sir?" Doctor Polidari shouted.

Harriman reached out a ham sized fist and knocked Doctor Polidari's hat from his head. Doctor Polidari stepped back and in one elegant motion drew his sword with a whoosh. The Highland officers moved toward the pair. Captain Thorpe was nearest the combatants.

"Draw, sir, draw!" Doctor Polidari cried. "Or I shall skewer you like the beast you are. Maximus! Take that fine young woman away, right away from here. You know what is said of pearls and swine!"

The two men circled one another with swords drawn, the Highland officers forming a line at a respectful distance from the duel. Captain Thorpe hastened up the steps and took Miriam's arm. He practically lifted her into the trap, took his seat, and started the horse in motion.

Miriam was incredulous Captain Thorpe should rush off and leave his friend. She turned round in her seat. Doctor Polidari dashed forward and in two quick passes opened Harriman's shirt front, making it blossom red. Then Miriam remembered: Dueling, Edinburgh.

"How fairs Polidari?" Captain Thorpe asked. "Has he killed his mon yet?"

Doctor Polidari emerged from a tight clench with Harriman. Harriman flew backward, landed on his back, and found the Doctor's foot on his wounded chest and a sharp sword point at his throat.

Miriam faced forward on her seat.

"He will no kill the brute," Captain Thorpe said. "Don't let that trouble you. Polidari is a medical man. Harriman shall have to beg the good doctor's pardon, and if he don't, well..."

"Then it shall be Harriman in the hole," Miriam said.

Captain Thorpe laughed aloud, one bark of laughter only before he contained himself. Thinking perhaps of the bloody encounter left behind, he said gravely, "There would be justice, Harriman in his own hell hole of a prison. But that shall never happen, he would have to change his skin colour, or this country would have to change entirely." Captain Thorpe paused, and glanced at Miriam out of the corner of his eye. "Pardon me for using course language, Miss Miriam, and indeed for bringing you into unfit company to-day."

Miriam hardly knew what to say, he didn't know the half of it. And why they—Captain Thorpe and Mr. Dashwood —should feel responsible for any of it, or for her, both puzzled and annoyed her.

"Stop the carriage, if you please, Captain!"

The horse was moving at a steady pace, but Captain Thorpe easily brought the animal up. They'd arrived at the outermost edge of Harriman's Hole, near the part of the corral where the women and children were earlier. Miriam stood up in the trap and scanned the enclosure, spotting the little group in the shade cast by the late afternoon sun behind the fencing.

"I had hoped to reach them from here," Miriam said, and then jumped down from the carriage.

"Hold hard, Miss," Captain Thorpe called after her. "What are you about?"

Miriam moved past an unoccupied guard tower, until she was level with the women and children. Taking from her reticule one of the rolls stuffed with lamb, Miriam hurled it over the fence. There was a startled cry from the group of women and children, and then shouts were heard in the distance.

Captain Thorpe sprang up beside her. "Give those to me," he said, "you throw like a little wee lassie."

She pulled the oranges and bread rolls from her bag, and Captain Thorpe fired them over the fence. Miriam studied the action of his throwing arm.

"Now, Miss, run! Look, as they are doing." Captain Thorpe pointed to the group running away with their morsels, to a remoter part of the yard.

Miriam sprang unladylike onto the carriage seat. Captain Thorpe followed and flicked the reins over the horse. Someone shouted at them in a guttural tone. As they passed, a string of bedraggled men filed out of the main building of Harriman's Hole and into the corral toward the horrible triangles and posts. The women and children might be able to eat their small portions, while the guards were distracted with beating their husbands, fathers, or brothers.

"Thank you, Captain Thorpe, I am obliged to you. I do throw like a...lassie."

"You must forgive me, I was in an agony lest the horse wander away and we afoot in this god forsaken country."

"You will be happy to return to *Nonesuch*," Miriam said. After a moment's hesitation, during which he seemed to hold his breath beside her, she added with perfect truth, "And so shall I."

It was a companionable return journey until they reached Cape Town. Captain Thorpe's posture suddenly stiffened as they drove past the Lutheran Church and the public library, painted white, yellow, and green, with a profusion of frolicking wooden gods and goddesses decorating the gable above a balustrade. A clear view of the anchorage in Table Bay opened up to them.

They left the horse and trap with its owner, one Mr. Strombom, and proceeded on foot. Unhappy rumbling noises were escaping Captain Thorpe, as they passed a gallows erected near the parade ground before the quay. Purple-black clouds tinged the color of tea at the edges were racing toward Cape Town and Table Bay, filling the sky from far out in the Atlantic. The weather had turned threatening, and so had Captain Thorpe's mood. Miriam couldn't account for the change in the affable companion of earlier, to the man walking beside her with clenched jaw, and a kindled, almost furious look in his mismatched eyes.

Captain Thorpe's gaze was concentrated on the ships at anchor. Miriam saw nothing unusual in the scene nor in *Nonesuch*, the ship's true character was well hidden. Indeed to her, there was a great deal of beauty in the sight of *Nonesuch* and the other ships in the Bay. But he was turning red in the face as they hustled toward the quay. Wearily, Miriam wondered if there was to be more bloodshed this day.

She was determined not to interfere, to refrain from asking what was vexing him. She would be silent, be modest, and hope she would not be the one Captain Thorpe blew up on.

"He is flying the Blue Peter!" Captain Thorpe cried, when *Nonesuch* was in full view. "Do you see, Miss Miriam, the blue flag with a white rectangle at its centre? Hoisting that signal means the ship is ready to sail. It is done to recall all hands, something only the ship's captain may order. Your Mr. Dashwood overreaches, so he does."

"He is not my Mr. Dashwood." Miriam replied, before she'd fully considered.

"Nay?" Captain Thorpe halted in his headlong rush to the ship. He turned to her, quite a changed expression on his face, the storm clouds receding.

"Perhaps this blue flag is only due to the weather," Miriam said.

Captain Thorpe tilted his head back and studied the sky and clouds, then squinted at her. "Oh aye, the weather. Did ye think I had not noticed?"

After saying this in a kind, almost jovial tone, Captain Thorpe offered Miriam his arm. They proceeded at a gentler pace to the quay, Miriam unsure what took the sting out of that blue peter.

CHAPTER NINE

Maximus's head ached from the long weary day, and the effort of restraining himself from cuffing Mr. Dashwood about the ears.

"I have great respect for your abilities as a navigator, Mr. Dashwood, and for your skill with the Mechanism," Maximus said. "What you will not be considering is the terrible cold it is rounding the Cape of Good Hope."

"But the lift, sir, this storm promises—"

"Aye. The ascent will be a thing of beauty. And once we are aloft, the flotation will ice over and we shall come down like a lead balloon, throwing out the guns, stores, and the buckles of our shoes to slow our crash." Maximus grimaced and motioned with his head. Miriam sat on the stern lockers, her back half turned as though she was not attending to their conversation. She drew Thrax closer to her.

"I beg your pardon, sir," Mr. Dashwood said, following the direction of Maximus's concerned gaze. "I had not considered—"

"No, indeed, Mr. Dashwood, I perceive you had not. May I just mention that if ever you have a notion to fly the Blue Peter at *Nonesuch's* masthead again without her captain aboard, there shall be consequences."

"Aye, aye, sir." Mr. Dashwood flushed and stared at his own pair of silver buckled shoes.

Maximus heaved a great sigh, disliking the tension and constraint between them. "In this instance it is almost fortunate you did fly the Blue Peter, Mr. Dashwood," he said.

"For if we don't up anchor and away this very moment, we shall find ourselves trapped in Table Bay."

Miriam rose and crossed the cabin with Thrax in her arms. After curtseying to them both she turned to enter her sleeping cabin, touching noses with Thrax and then kissing the top of the furry head.

Maximus felt like he'd been hit in the bread basket with the business end of a cudgel. It was a long time since anyone kissed him. He gave a little ahem. "Time won't wait, nor tide show mercy, Mr. Dashwood. Let us be about it."

Mr. Dashwood had to admit that Captain Thorpe was right; rounding the Cape of Good Hope it was one squall after another, bringing heavy rain and sleet. Once round the Cape though, he was able to guide them reading the Mechanism as no one else could do—or so he fancied—into the southern Indian Ocean. This was Mr. Dashwood's third aerial cruise. The second one was when they'd ascended in the vicinity of the islands of Amsterdam and St. Paul, those remote volcanic island outcroppings stuffed with seals, penguins, and mermaids. The ship was carried at a tremendous rate by the variables from there to Van Diem's land and New South Wales.

Nonesuch put into Port Jackson to rest and re-fuel. Excepting wood for the braziers, the ship didn't desire much in the way of stores since their transits were of short duration. Captain Thorpe was a great one for resting his crew, however, and so they made themselves look respectable and called on Port Jackson. They need not have bothered. The captain went ashore and after viewing the squalor of the place, returned muttering in his broad Scottish brogue about "dirty and rubbishy going together" and hurried the wood and water aboard. His lady guest Captain Thorpe rowed to a headland outside the town so that Miriam could stretch her legs on dry land amid flocks of parrots, cockatiels, and budgerigars, and away from the sight of the criminals, sots, and blackguards in Port Jackson.

This same tender inclination, Mr. Dashwood believed, led Captain Thorpe to allow Miriam to remain on *Nonesuch's* upper deck during their present descent. If Mr. Dashwood's readings were correct this third landing should put them in the Celebes Sea, or even into the South China Sea itself.

Mr. Dashwood was beginning to suspect he'd misjudged Miriam, and she had less in her of the gentlewoman and more of the adventuress, for there were signs she returned the captain's sentiments. He was surprised she should favor Captain Thorpe in spite of his cautionary words in Cape Town, to say nothing of his own very nearly expressed preference for her. Most of all he could not approve of allowing a woman to remain on deck during a dangerous maneuver like a descent. At the same time, as first lieutenant, Mr. Dashwood felt it beneath his dignity to notice her.

Miriam was strapped aft, to a stanchion of the quarterdeck, out of the way of the working of the bellows, the braziers, the lines of the balloons, and the critical ballast. Dashwood thought her an absurd sight in her trowsers, head scarf, and knitted cap tied beneath her chin, held to the stanchion and lifelines by a canvas jacket arrangement with buckles and latches of Captain Thorpe's own devising.

"Let go the hundred-weights, port and starboard!" Mr. Dashwood called.

Nonesuch's descent slowed and she lifted in a gentle upward swoop and then dipped through another thin layer of cloud. Below them stretched a pacific sea with never a white cap in sight. The night was beautifully starlit, and even at altitude the air temperature nearly comfortable. Mr. Dashwood was confident this would be his prettiest landing yet, and that it should take place before Miss Miriam's eyes didn't detract from his joy.

The ship gave an awkward gripe when *Nonesuch* was some hundred feet above the water, listing horribly to starboard. The balloons were nearing complete deflation and had not Mr. Dashwood instantly called an adjustment to the men manning the stunsail sheets the ship might have rolled over. For several tense seconds she felt sickeningly near to going masts down. What flashed through Mr. Dashwood's mind was, Captain Thorpe's uncommon zeal for the passenger on deck caused the split second loss of control. No man ever held helm that did not some time lose his hold, Mr. Dashwood reflected. An error like that might've cost them dear.

Next moment the ship was down and boisterous over a calm sea. Mr. Dashwood began shouting orders to bring the ship to, to house the wind-engine and fix her rudder, to furl in and secure the flotation, setting in motion the myriad tasks of a landing.

"Mr. Dashwood, sir," Miriam called to him from aft. "There are three vessels coming up fast."

When Mr. Dashwood scanned the sea round he spotted them. Three Chinese junks, their large mat sails set, wringing great speed out of the slight breeze and on a course to intercept *Nonesuch*.

"Arm yourselves!" Mr. Dashwood called out to the men on deck.

He ran back to Miriam, unhooking her from lifeline and stanchion until she stood swaying before him, all canvas jacket and dangling buckles.

"Run below, Miss. Tell the Captain we are about to be boarded."

Miriam hurried for the companion ladder, but up it rushed a file of shrieking men, with Captain Thorpe at their head. He had his sword in his hand, pistols in belts across his chest, and such a furious maniacal grin on his face that Miriam fell back to the stanchion on the quarterdeck.

Over the sides of the ship hung the two great limp balloons, blocking both gangways with the complicated lines that secured them to the ship. Miriam could hear cries from the forecastle where the pirates had boarded, Mr. Dashwood and his men were struggling over those lines to meet them. It was to be the British cutlass and cavalry swords against the native *parang* and *kris*.

Miriam ran again for the after hatchway companion ladder to retreat below deck. But a hand grasped her roughly by the canvas jacket she still wore and shoved her into place with the afterguard, hauling on lines to bring in a balloon.

"Where do you think you're a going to, mate?" the owner of the hand shouted at her. "Captain orders the flotations brought in, and you think it's time to go below and take a caulk?"

She'd watched them do this before, the united pulling upon the lines, the furling and folding of the great balloons. Miriam did her best not to squib their rhythm, but the balloon grew ever heavier with the weight of water. From forward on deck came the sound of clashing swords, and the fearful screams and groans of battle.

"Braziers, light the braziers."

Miriam heard Captain Thorpe's cry as the afterguard finished furling one balloon on the deck. Captain Thorpe was amidships, his sword back in the scabbard at his hip. He called out for the bellows to be manned. Several of the afterguard rushed to take up stations, while Miriam with the rest made their way to the port side balloon. A Chinese junk came round *Nonesuch's* stern, tossing stink pots up on her deck.

"Oh no you didn't!" Captain Thorpe roared, running aft and kicking the smoking bombs over the ship's side.

"Mr. Dashwood! On my word fall back to the quarterdeck!"

The port side balloon was furled double quick, and Captain Thorpe called out for the gangways to be cleared.

Miriam moved away with the hands, to huddle near the lee rail. Jugma Bora was close by. She was looking right at him when Bora made a come hither gesture at the Chinese junk making itself fast to *Nonesuch,* in preparation for boarding her over the stern.

She opened her mouth to give warning of this second wave of pirates attacking the ship. But forward Captain Thorpe was shouting orders, recalling Mr. Dashwood and the watch on deck. When they leaped past him, Captain Thorpe ordered the bellows directed over the flames of the braziers. The pirates left on the forecastle were blasted from the ship.

A cheer went up from *Nonesuch's* crew.

Captain Thorpe was having none of it. "Firemen!" he shouted.

Into the momentary hush after this command, amid the rush forward of the men called, Miriam shouted. "Arm yourselves! We are about to be boarded up in here."

In the charge of seamen as the crew came pounding aft to deal with the raiders clawing at the stern, Miriam was pushed all the way to the taffrail. She felt a calloused hand close on her wrist. Jugma Bora had her in a hard clasp.

"Little Dragon!" called a man with blackened teeth, looking up at them from the deck of the junk. "What are you doing with the *farang?*"

Miriam stared, wondering if she'd understood the eastern language quite so well. She and Jugma Bora turned to one another, and Miriam found her answer in his cold gaze.

"Here's the one you want! She's a British spy and will fetch a fine ransom."

Jugma Bora jerked Miriam's hand up, or tried to. She resisted the man who'd lulled her with tales of another woman's success, pulling and twisting her wrist painfully in his grasp.

"You will be letting her loose now, Bora, as you value your life."

Shouts and cries engulfed them as the Nonesuches repelled pirates from the quarterdeck, yet Miriam heard that Scottish burr quite clear in the melee. Grappling hand to hand, she and Jugma Bora staggered together and apart, nearly crashing into Captain Thorpe. He held a pistol cocked and pointed. Captain Thorpe came face to face with Jugma Bora, raised a booted foot, and kicked him square in the chest.

Miriam reeled back as someone caught her round the waist. Jugma Bora tumbled over the taffrail, smacking into two of his kinsmen on his way down and knocking them from the stern ladder.

Saramago was the one who'd held onto her. He peered at her, shaking his head, his eyes misting over. "And you always so kind and polite to that Bora."

"Here you are, Miss." Captain Thorpe put a three and half inch blade into her hand, the Scottish *sgian dubh*. "And may you never more be without it. Mr. Dashwood, sway up one of the guns, I grow tired of vermin on my ship!"

It was not the swivel gun that saved them from further assault, but a wind coming up. Mr. Dashwood was fixing one of the guns to its carriage, the Chinese junks having fallen back to regroup, when a fair land breeze from the nearby islands found them. Captain Thorpe roared orders that set the sails on his polymorphous craft, and *Nonesuch* showed the three junks her heels.

"Well, Valentine," Maximus said to his first lieutenant late that evening, "those are the dangers of descending in fair weather." They were reclining at table in the great cabin, having attended to repairs to the ship and to her people. Maximus spent some considerable time stitching knife wounds, and sewing ears back on. "Particularly in these seas, with pirates round every coral reef. We shall have to practice swaying up the guns, when the men are sufficiently recovered."

"I much doubt we shall find weather favorable for an ascent, sir," Mr. Dashwood said, "among these islands, and in this latitude. At least, that is my reading of the Mechanism thus far."

Maximus nodded, trying to look grave and not pleased to extend the time before *Nonesuch* should reach Hong Kong. Miss Miriam had assisted him with the wounded like a regular surgeon's mate, having benefited from his anatomical instruction. He was not unaware either of how she'd behaved during the late action, shoved about on deck by the bosun, working with the afterguard. *Nonesuch's* bosun Mr. Wagner was a perfect Bruin; Maximus made a mental note to discuss with him the difference between a landsman and a young lady.

"That's as may be," Maximus said. "Once we are in the South China Sea, we may find squalls. Relieve Mr. Dodd at eight bells, and I shall take the morning watch."

"Aye, aye, sir." Mr. Dashwood rose. "By the way, sir, may I say that caper with the bellows and the braziers made things rather *hot* for the natives."

"Mr. Dashwood, I cannot but be approving of a first lieutenant who doesn't care overmuch for the gingerbread-work."

"Good night, sir." Mr. Dashwood walked out grinning.

Maximus was dead tired and he went and had a wash in the quarter gallery. He returned to the great cabin shirtless, and there found Miriam with her long dark hair in a plait over one shoulder, wearing a dressing gown and list slippers.

"I shall be with you in a trice," he cried, scurrying into his sleeping cabin and emerging a moment later wearing a fresh shirt.

The sight of her, so obviously ready for bed, moved Maximus in many ways. She was at once innocent and alluring. Miriam stood with her dark gaze cast down. Though she had not blushed to see his naked chest, she seemed now to be having trouble meeting his eye. Maximus hoped he hadn't given her a disgust of him with his pale skin, and his curling red gold chest hair.

It was a relief when she spoke first.

"I am sorry to keep you from your cot, Captain, I know it has been a most difficult day. I could not rest because I...did you hear what he called me?"

"That traitor Bora?"

Miriam nodded. "If you understood as well as I did, Jugma Bora may be a betrayer but he is also a prodigious great teacher. He called me a spy. A British spy."

Her fear, her distress, and uncertainty were plain. Maximus's strongest instinct urged him to protect her.

"No one can like the name of agent provocateur," Maximus said. "If Bora survived this day to spread that tale far and wide, sure you must reconsider carrying on with your mission."

He was sorry to be so blunt. Miriam's skin was near green-tinged she was so pale. Maximus found he should do anything to persuade her to abandon Lord Q's infamous, ill-conceived attempt at rescue. Or was it a bait and switch? The notion made Maximus grit his teeth.

"He called Jugma Bora Little Dragon. Did you attend to it?"

Miriam turned those luminous intelligent eyes on him, and Maximus's throat went dry. "So I did too," he croaked.

"The Golden Dragon and Little Dragon," she said. "Do you think Lord Exmouth can have unwittingly sent his own agent provocateur aboard with us? It is hardly likely. I cannot help but feel we may have tossed overboard his lordship's man on the inside of this clan abducting women."

Maximus rubbed his hands over his weary beard stubbled face. "At this moment I am too tired to ken who is doing what to whom, Miss, I hope you will forgive me. Allow me to say the only thing I know is, the middle of a criminal conspiracy is no place for a gentle lass like you."

He meant only to be complimentary and honest, but at once Maximus realized he'd blundered again, and invaded the space she liked to keep round herself. Miriam's gaze became hard and abstracted, and then she stood up.

"Good night, sir, and thank you for allowing me to remain on deck during the descent. It was the most glorious night of my life, until we were attacked."

"Thank you, ma'am, for your service to the ship and her people." Maximus bowed, pained by this formality between them—a self-inflicted wound.

"Tell me, Captain," Miriam said, moving to the door of her sleeping cabin. "Why did you not let them take me, those pirates who attacked the ship? Since that is what is meant to happen."

"I have my orders, which are to set you down in Hong Kong. Not to hand you over to the first pointy toothed bugger who crawls up the side."

"Ah! Orders," Miriam said. She dipped him a little curtsey. "And so you will understand that I too have mine."

CHAPTER TEN

Beautiful verdant islands slipped by on both sides of *Nonesuch*. The offshore breezes brought the scent of flowers, moist earth, and exuberant vegetable life. Brilliant colored birds —flocks of lories, hornbills, and parrots—shrieked from the forrest canopies. Native longhouses appeared where the jungle had been cleared, and many were built extending out over the water. Miriam couldn't truly enjoy these fascinating sights, though she was much on deck. When they gained the South China Sea and *Nonesuch* was obliged to beat against contrary winds and a boisterous sea, the weather better suited Miriam's mood. A sense of dread plagued her, the same as she'd experienced before leaving her mother and Iran.

Here was that feeling again, unwelcome and unwanted, of living her last days of peaceful untroubled existence, of time running short. Miriam was angry that she'd wound up in the same place, though in a far distant tropical landscape, whose natural wonders she couldn't appreciate for her anxiety and depression of spirit. She worried over what became of Jugma Bora, and about her fast approaching meeting with Francis Blackwell. The greater part of Miriam's unhappiness though, stemmed from losing what had come to feel like a home. The ship *Nonesuch*, with Captain Thorpe and—she had to admit it—the officers and crew, substituting for a family.

Since Africa Mr. Dashwood had called a halt to his offers of gifts and guidance, and Miriam liked him better for it. He now quizzed her, full of good-humored raillery, and Saramago doted on her. Mr. Dodd and the heavy-handed bosun Mr. Wagner had each on occasion treated her chuff, just like brothers. And Captain Thorpe? She would actually miss those odd mismatched eyes, and his gallant ways. Miriam was disappointed he wouldn't help her unravel what had happened with Jugma Bora. Captain Thorpe must know Lord Exmouth better than she, but he didn't care to share that knowledge. He seemed to believe Miriam needed to be handled with especial care and wrapped in lamb's wool.

In spite of the wishes of many more aboard *Nonesuch* than Miriam was aware, the ship came in to the fine harbor of Hong Kong at last. Dutch, British, and American ships great and small, and junks, *prahus*, and *kora-kora* crowded the port. *Nonesuch* was brought safely to anchor by her attentive officers and crew, amid the crowd of vessels and house-boats. Miriam stood on *Nonesuch's* deck taking in the settlement and the mountainous terrain. The town consisted of a patchwork of warehouses, counting and merchant houses, and residences at the foot, and running a short way up a misty hillside. Somewhere in the humid little town her step-father Francis would be sweating at the British Consulate.

The day she was to leave the ship Miriam felt oppressed, and not just by the climate. Her basket containing her few possessions was in the great cabin, ready to be put into the boat that would carry her ashore. On the quay Miriam planned to hire a palanquin or sedan chair to take her to Government House. That was how everyone got around, even to visit their next-door neighbor, on the steep streets of the settlement. She stood in the great cabin wringing her hands, tarted up in Lady Elgin's clothes, with her hair dressed and uncovered. Miriam was anxious; Thrax hadn't been around all morning.

"No, Miss, I no see 'em," Saramago answered her inquiry.

"Pisamdeared again," Miriam said. "And I must say good-bye soon."

She and Saramago were blinking at one another with moist eyes, when Captain Thorpe entered from his private quarters. He left the door to his bed space open, a thing Miriam never knew him do before, and she was able to gaze into luxury and comfort.

"May I beg a private word with ye, Miss Miriam," Captain Thorpe said.

Saramago melted away, muttering that he would go hunt down the Hell-Cat.

Captain Thorpe and Miriam took seats in the great cabin, just as on so many other occasions. This time there was an especial tension between them, one that had been building since their descent into dangerous waters.

"How I hope Thrax may turn up soon," Miriam said, clasping her hands together in her lap. "I must leave for Government House at half past the hour."

"Just so," Captain Thorpe said. "I hope Thrax will no be the only one you will be missing, Miss Miriam. If you choose to go, I mean to say. I was wanting to speak to you, to convince you not to leave the ship."

Miriam frowned. "This is the mission, sir, the duty I've been given by your government. You would have me come all this way, and balk at the last?"

"I would. I would indeed," Captain Thorpe said. "Marry me, stay aboard my ship, and you will be answerable to no man."

The unexpected offer hit Miriam hard. The first thought that shot through her brain was, *answerable to no man but you*. Miriam realized she might be doing Captain Thorpe an injustice. She was stunned, and in grasping for a response Miriam realized he'd not spoken of love.

"You do me a very great honor," Miriam said. "I am sensible of your goodness, in wishing to protect me from...But if I were to accept, would not that answer your kindness by bringing down on your head the wrath of your superiors?"

A strange look came into Captain Thorpe's eyes, and he lifted his chin. "Scotsmen are notorious proud, Miss Miriam, and I will have you know I consider no English man my superior. A horn in the sides of Lords Exmouth and Q if it don't please them. Crack ship captains are not so easy to come by."

Captain Thorpe smiled at Miriam as though he'd surmounted the greatest objection she could discover to his proposal. Miriam felt weak and a bit lightheaded, because of the heat and anxiety of the last days—and now this. She found she wanted to say yes, yes with all her heart, to staying aboard *Nonesuch*, the home she'd been so bitterly regretting having to give up. She need not venture into the fearful unknown, or go ashore to the dreaded meeting with Francis. They might go together to meet her step-father, make their announcement, and let the communication of her desertion of her British masters be his problem. There would be some justice in that. Meanwhile she and Captain Thorpe would be floating hundreds of leagues away in the sparkling ether.

Miriam shook her head, to clear it of self-deluding dreams. "I dare say you are right, and you at least shall be forgiven any transgression. May I ask, pardon me if this seems obvious to you, what would become of me after the nuptials? Should I go to live with your relations in Scotland?"

Confusion clouded Captain Thorpe's face. "Aye, aye, of course. That is what a gentlewoman would expect, no doubt."

Miriam bowed her head, trying to conceal her disappointment. How to find the words? She had a great fondness for him, and more than that respected and esteemed Captain Thorpe.

"It is hard for me to express how grateful I am for your kind and generous offer, but I must decline. My conscience urges me not to give up on the mission your government has entrusted to me, to help those women."

"Who are they to you?" Captain Thorpe burst out. "They are no your mother, or your sisters!"

His passion surprised Miriam, though the injury and pain in his eyes should have warned her of a squall.

"I know that. I do not venture into this because they are my sisters, or some fantasy of a better mother than the one I have." Miriam paused a moment, a little shocked at that idea. "I do it because they are people, like you and me."

Captain Thorpe was hunched forward in his chair, leaning toward her with his forearms resting on his knees.

"One person to another, then, Miss Miriam. Tell me what it is you want, and I shall be happy to oblige. Even if you wish me to bugger off back to Scotland."

A little laugh escaped her, but Miriam's heart was wrung. Lately she barely noticed those unnatural eyes, except when they were alive with strong emotion.

"One person to another then, my dear sir, I can only tell you what it is I don't want. I don't want to have to give an accounting of myself, and be told where I may go, and what I may and may not do. I don't want to be told what I should value, who I should love, or what God to address in my prayers."

Miriam paused to blot tears from her face with her handkerchief. She breathed a great sigh, to think this day was only just beginning. "Now it is your turn, Captain Thorpe. If you are not too offended with me, tell me what it is you want."

His expression was serious and considering. Captain Thorpe looked straight at her. "Not to be judged," he said.

The great cabin door opened and Thrax darted in ahead of Saramago's foot. The steward shut the door on their private conference, after casting a knowing glance at the pair of them.

Miriam rose, feeling ineffably sad, and made to pick Thrax up and spend her love upon the Hell-Cat. Thrax evaded her, and jumped into the basket with Miriam's belongings. The animal burrowed down, while gazing up at her and Captain Thorpe.

"You may not come with me, Thrax, my dear," Miriam said.

"Why ever not?"

"I do not mean to make myself conspicuous. People may not remember an English speaking woman in China, but one sporting a lap dog or cat is another matter entirely."

"It seems to me you will be noticed in any case. At this point in your mission, I take it that is your intention." Captain Thorpe cast a worried glance at Miriam in her fancy dress. "I beg you will take the Hell-Cat, remember it is a fierce and loyal companion."

Thrax' eyes appeared too large for its head. The cat seemed to shrink in size before them, a timid innocuous little creature.

"I've never seen a cat simper before," Captain Thorpe said.

Miriam laughed, and her relief was so great she extended her hand to the Captain.

"I must certainly take Thrax. It was Megabazus' gift to you, and yours to me." Miriam retained her hold of Captain Thorpe's hand. Gazing past him into his book lined private haven, Miriam was reminded of those lines of poetry.

> Since in this heart he sought love of a friend,
> Know that in that heart love will be sustained.

"In my country we have what is called *sigheh*," Miriam said. "It means temporary wife. I will put my trust in the British exit strategy, and when I return—" she would not say *if*, "when the mission is done, I will be *sigheh* to you. If your wishes are unchanged."

She watched the emotion on Captain Thorpe's face change from rejection and disappointment, to surprise, and then came tenderness and even joy.

"Don't give me your answer just yet," Miriam hastened to say, when she saw him ready to commit himself. "Think over whether you can accept such a difficult, demanding, contrary woman, I beg. When we meet again after...then you may tell me."

Captain Thorpe lifted her hand to his lips and kissed it. An unexpected thrill ran through Miriam, culminating in a fluttering at her core.

She withdrew her hand rather shakily from his grasp. "Perhaps you will be good enough to see me ashore, Captain?" Miriam went over and took her basket on her arm.

CHAPTER ELEVEN

Francis Blackwell dreaded the meeting with Miriam in the way a man does when he believes he's done another an ill turn. How much worse one felt when that other person was female, and under your protection, Francis knew only too well. He'd been astonished when word of her arrival in Hong Kong was brought him by HMHV *Nonesuch*, and even more confounded by the content of letters sent via that ship. One was from Lord Q, under cover of another letter from Sir Edward Pellew. Francis went about his assigned diplomatic task of hiring passage on a San Francisco bound vessel for Miriam in a sort of dream, or in truth, a nightmarish haze.

Miriam swept into the British Consul in Hong Kong's private office on the arm of Captain Thorpe. She registered the surprise on Francis's face to see her dressed as she was, on the arm of a Navy officer. It pleased her that Francis should behold her changed from the timid person he'd left behind in Iran to face charges of improper conduct on her own.

"Uncle." Miriam addressed Francis respectfully, as she'd been taught to do. Gritting her teeth, Miriam moved around his desk to embrace him. "How do you do? Allow me to present Captain Maximus Thorpe, of *Nonesuch*. Captain Thorpe, my—, His Majesty's consul in Hong Kong, Mr. Francis Blackwell."

The men exchanged how do you do's, and Francis invited them to sit down. Miriam was infinitely glad of Captain Thorpe's presence, the situation was awkward enough, it would have been intolerable to be alone with Francis. Did that make her more like the timid self she'd tried to leave behind than she wanted to believe?

"And so you've come all this way in a crack ship, Miriam?" Francis said.

Not, how is your mother, how is your brother, how are you, Miriam? If that was the way it was to be between them, she was not unwilling.

"Only to turn round and sail back again," she said in a cold tone. "Across the Pacific, this time."

"I appeal to you, Captain Thorpe, as Lord Exmouth informs me you know all and are part of his exit strategy. Is not this a most pernicious scheme Miriam has entangled herself in?"

What answer Captain Thorpe might have made they did not find out, because Miriam said, "Pernicious, sir? Should you like to know how I came to the notice of a man like Lord Q? How I came to be indebted to the British, and involved in pernicious schemes?"

Francis Blackwell blanched visibly. "Perhaps Captain Thorpe has business he would like to attend to in town, and then you and I can have a private discussion."

"I am obliged to you, sir," Captain Thorpe said. "But I won't be taking my leave unless and until Miss Miriam invites me to do so."

During this brief exchange Miriam thought better of making any accusations. She'd been on the point of blaming Francis for her acquaintance with Lords Exmouth and Q; that was true enough, she would not have known them but for moving in Francis's diplomatic circles. But it was not in the least true that she was there in Hong Kong ready to take part in what he called pernicious schemes, and she called trying to help other women, because of him. At worst he was guilty of having run, of insufficient courage in facing the backlash of scandal that linked them together in criminal congress.

"I should like to know, Uncle," Miriam said, "of the ship and passage you've arranged for me. And about the lodging I am to take up here in Hong Kong, if you please. I'm sure I have imposed long enough on Captain Thorpe's hospitality."

"Not in the least," Captain Thorpe said, an arch expression spreading over his weather-beaten face. "If the lodgings your *uncle* has arranged do not suit, or you are in the least uncomfortable, you must return to *Nonesuch* at once. The entire crew shall welcome you back aboard as one of their own."

This last Captain Thorpe said directly to Francis Blackwell.

The lodgings Francis found for Miriam did suit, as she discovered when taken round to them that first day ashore by both her step-father and Captain Thorpe. It was in the home of a merchant, the supercargo of the ship *Caldera* that Miriam was to take passage in. Goh Cheng Cheng was a man of fifty, a man of substance, the owner of several warehouses in San Francisco and Canton, who opened his part-Eastern, part-Western establishment to the British Consul's honored guest. Miriam had to admit Francis knew his business as a diplomat, and wasn't at all unwilling to spend lavishly on her comfort.

During her stay in Goh Cheng Cheng's house, it was inevitable that Francis should sometime find her alone. One morning Goh Cheng Cheng, who was aware of and cooperating in the British counter-piracy plan, led Francis Blackwell through the large and complex dwelling to Miriam's apartments rather than entrusting him to a servant.

Miriam turned round from where she sat in her bedchamber before a dressing table. "Uncle Francis, how kind in you to call so early."

Goh Cheng Cheng bowed and took his leave. Francis seated himself without an invitation.

"You will forgive me for calling on you before the usual hour," he said, "but I wished to speak to you alone. We both know I have far more to beg your pardon for than just an untimely visit."

"Shall we walk in the gardens?" Miriam said, glancing round her apartment. It was a beautiful and intimate room filled with blossoms, musical instruments, lacquered furniture, ancient art, and opium-pipes and cigarettes. "I never expected to see such fine gardens in an outpost like Hong Kong."

"I should be offended for my new home town," Francis said, rising from his chair.

The complex was surrounded by verandahs both outward facing toward the street where business was often transacted, and leading from the interior rooms on to enclosed gardens. Miriam and Francis passed through apartments where lanterns of different shapes and materials hung from the ceilings, made of glass, gauze, and colored paper, with shades fringed, tufted, and bedecked with bells. Beyond carved wooden screens through which the perfume of tropical flowers, the scent and bird song of the outdoors drifted into the interior of the house, they descended the verandah steps into the maze of gardens.

After pacing a short ways, Francis said, "Before this kingdom in miniature and by all that's holy, Miriam, my intention was never to hurt you, nor see you indebted to Lord Q. I left because I—" There was a hitch in Francis's voice, and he paused. They were surrounded by perfect little worlds with grottos, rivulets and pools, and small stone castles atop miniature mountains. "I was a coward, and so wounded by Zahraa taking up with that Prancer—"

"Did you know Mama wants to marry me to Haris Reza? Solves everything, for her at least. She would have Haris, and I would keep my good name."

"Oh, Miriam!"

"You may well exclaim. I went to Lord Q, and then I ran, just like you."

Francis halted beside a pond where orange and black and white carp swam in the shadows round the pool's edge.

"Everyone knew you were my favorite, I was always so proud of you," he said. "And then to have my fondness for you become suspect, to be accused of taking advantage of you..." Francis shook his head. They'd sat down on a stone bench beside the pond. "It was unthinkable and in my confusion of spirit I decided the best thing I could do, was to leave."

Despite the tranquil setting, Miriam felt belligerent. "Best for who exactly, Uncle?"

Francis winced. "You would oblige me ever so much if you would just call me Francis. With all my heart I beg your forgiveness. Maybe I should have stayed, and tried to face down Zahraa and her schemes."

Miriam stood abruptly and with a rapid stride started down the gravel path.

Francis hastened after her. "Most of all," he said, "I didn't want to be the one...I couldn't bear to be there when you realized—"

"It was Mama started those rumors, about you and me?" Pain gripped Miriam's heart as she uttered those words, and saw the truth confirmed in Francis's gaze.

She slowed her pace, the footpath becoming blurry because of her tears. The track wound round the base of a hill forested with flowering shrubs. Ahead on the path, they both caught a glimpse of the rich garments of a lady fleeing on unnaturally small feet.

"One of Goh Cheng Cheng's harem," Francis said. They stopped to allow the woman to make good her retreat.

Miriam sniffed and searched in the pocket of her gown for a handkerchief. "I wonder how long I would need to be here, before I could be permitted to visit Goh Cheng Cheng's wives and daughters."

Francis handed her his own handkerchief, and as Miriam dabbed at the tears and moisture on her skin, he said in a gentle tone, "Merry, my dear, family relations are complicated. That might take generations."

Miriam didn't have a lifetime to wait. After passing a few tranquil days at Goh Cheng Cheng's establishment, visited everyday by the people of *Nonesuch* and the British Consul, she was summoned aboard *Caldera*. Miriam, Francis Blackwell, and Captain Thorpe had agreed that Captain Thorpe alone would see Miriam aboard the merchant ship. Francis could not appear and give *Caldera's* commander, Captain Clooney, nor anyone else, a whiff of the foreign office. Captain Clooney had fallen victim to pirates once before in the South China Sea, according to Francis, and *Caldera* sailed like a slug. These reasons for choosing *Caldera* for the mission naturally couldn't be revealed to her captain. Captain Clooney was given to understand Miriam was an English speaking lady, possibly of European descent, traveling to San Francisco on the advice of her physician.

On a muggy overcast morning Miriam boarded *Caldera* with her own personal medico at her side. Wearing a black frock coat and disreputable bob wig pinned to a rusty misshapen hat, with green spectacles to conceal his eyes, Captain Thorpe glanced round *Caldera's* disorderly deck and sniffed in a disdainful way. Together they sought out Captain Clooney, weaving round bails of tea, chickens stacked in wooden crates, and untidy coils of line that made Captain Thorpe shake his head. A low, vaguely Scottish sounding noise of disapproval kept coming out of him. They succeeded in finding the captain's steward, who conducted them to Miriam's assigned berth.

"Well now, Miss Blackwell," Captain Thorpe said in an officious tone, while *Caldera's* steward stood in the cabin doorway gaping, "it will be no indoor journey. No indeed, all the way across the Pacific to San Francisco, but you must undertake it, so you must."

In the cramped cabin was a wooden berth where Captain Thorpe tossed the bundle of mattress, blankets, and pillows he'd carried in for Miriam. A low writing table combined with a wash handstand completed the furnishings. Miriam set her basket, with Thrax perched atop her belongings, on the deck.

"That will be all, my mon." With a show of reluctance Captain Thorpe eased sixpence out of his pocket and put the pennies in the steward's hand. "The young person suffers from the falling damps," he said, in a confidential tone to the steward. "She must escape the humid air or I shall not answer for her constitution."

The steward shook his head with a withering look in Captain Thorpe's direction, and closed his fist around the coins. As the steward withdrew, Thrax leaped from Miriam's basket and slid out the cabin door.

Thrax leaving, and something in the set of Captain Thorpe's shoulders as he leaned over to close the cabin door, warned Miriam of an attack. In one practiced motion she lifted her skirt and withdrew the three and half inch blade from her stocking, meeting Captain Thorpe in a fighting stance, with the *sgian dubh* held firmly in an underhand grip.

He lunged toward her and instead of backing away, Miriam stepped into him and drove the blade in its wooden sheath up toward Captain Thorpe's belly.

Captain Thorpe spun away to avoid the blow. "Well done, Miss," he whispered. "More force next time, a man's skin is tough like hide, tight like a drum. Thrust the knife in with all your weight behind it."

He came at her again and Miriam mimicked stabbing him on one side and then the other, underneath his last rib and up into his vital organs. It was perfectly understood that he could neither attack her realistically nor she defend fiercely, but they still went through the motions. At last they stood close together, both panting slightly from their exertions and the effort of fighting without making a sound.

"You have flipped your wig, Doctor," Miriam said.

Captain Thorpe snorted. It had come off first thing and lay on the deck like a strange hollowed out creature. He took her hand and led her to sit side by side with him on the berth.

"How I shall miss your good cheer," Captain Thorpe said, "and in truth, everything about you."

Miriam gave in to a desire to lean upon him, her head on his shoulder, their hands still clasped.

"Nay, I don't know how I am to part with you, nor keep from coming after you directly you sail."

The British strategy called for Captain Thorpe to wait a fortnight before following Miriam into the South China Sea, to give the pirates ample time to strike.

"I hope..." Miriam's throat went dry. She swallowed with difficulty. "With all my heart, I hope it will be a short separation. But there is no sense in supposing what may happen."

She looked down at their joined hands and began to gently pull hers away. Captain Thorpe did not resist.

He nodded his head. "We Scots say supposing is not sense, nor is talk love."

Miriam gripped his hand one last time and then let go. Captain Thorpe asked her to repeat the details of the exit strategy aloud—Navy fashion—and together they checked over the accoutrement that were part of the plan.

"You are a brave woman," Captain Thorpe said, his voice full of emotion. "Better not begin than stop without finishing, is your way of thinking. Stay alive, Miss Miriam, and I shall find you."

The attack happened at night and in light winds, just as when *Nonesuch* came down from that last glorious ascent. Miriam, lying fully clothed in her berth, heard the first shouts from the crew on deck, the sound of the pirate craft bumping against *Caldera*, and the thuds and guttural cries as the attackers gained her deck. A furious rapping started up on her cabin door. Miriam rose and flung the door open for Captain Clooney.

"God help us, Miss," Captain Clooney cried, rushing in. "It's happening again! Put these on and come with me. I can't believe it's happening again!"

He gave her a set of men's clothing, trowsers and jacket, to disguise herself as a ship's boy.

"Hurry, Miss, there's not much time. There are three great junks grappled to us! The watch on deck won't be able to keep off so many. If they spend their fury while we take refuge in the hold, we might go unmolested."

Miriam thanked Captain Clooney in a distracted halting way, and then stared purposefully at the door of her cabin.

"Oh! Yes, ma'am," he said, and hastened outside.

Thrax was perched on Miriam's berth, staring at her intently. Miriam pulled the trowsers on, tucked in the skirt of her gown, and secured the whole with a number of scarves knotted round her waist. She donned the jacket and gathered her hair beneath the cap Saramago made her. Miriam peered past Thrax at her reflection in a small square looking glass positioned above the cot. Thrax bumped her aside, and for a moment its reflection replaced her own in the glass. The animal lifted its lips and hissed with menacing intent.

They turned with one accord to the door. Miriam yanked it open and Thrax rushed out. The Hell-Cat was no larger in size as it disappeared into the bowels of the ship than the Hong Kong rats it used to bring into Goh Cheng Cheng's gardens. There it would sit happily crunching away, the perpetrator of a scene of gore in the most beautiful setting.

In the passage outside her cabin, it was not Captain Clooney but Goh Cheng Cheng that awaited her.

"You see why I do not countenance cats?" Goh Cheng Cheng jerked his head in the direction Thrax had pisamdeared, as Saramago would say. "This way, madam. The captain and the watch below did not feel they could wait longer, before hiding themselves in the hold."

Much good it did them. Goh Cheng Cheng led Miriam down and down, to the furthest recesses of the hold where the goods of his merchant house, as well as those of many others, was stacked and packed with great precision. Holding up a dark lantern, Goh Cheng Cheng guided Miriam to a hiding place among crated porcelains. Many pairs of wide eyes near them reflected the lantern light before Goh Cheng Cheng extinguished it.

An anxious wait ensued there in the dark, with the heavy respiration of frightened men round her, hoping the pirates would be too distracted to find and loot them. Miriam touched the dagger strapped in her half boot. Only in the last exigency did she feel she could use it. It was hot and airless in the hold.

Miriam suspected any resistance the crew on *Caldera's* deck offered the pirates was probably overcome by the time she and Goh Cheng Cheng were descending the ladders. Over their heads, in that calm sea, Miriam and her companions listened to a fearful carouse. It sounded as though the pirates were dancing and drinking, and throwing and dragging the furnishings about.

"What is going on?" she breathed to Goh Cheng Cheng.

"Just a little sport, madam, do not concern yourself," Goh Cheng Cheng replied in Cantonese, which Miriam understood thanks to Jugma Bora. "They will find us out soon enough. And take everything away."

Goh Cheng Cheng's resigned and despairing tone caused Miriam the first chill of fright. Why she wasn't afraid before this Miriam could not say, ass-like stupidity probably. Somehow the practical old merchant's cold certainly made clear to her the chaotic, dangerous situation she was in.

A half dozen men came noisily down the ladder to the hold, casting lantern light in wide circles round them, hooting as they found each new section of goods. Tea, silks, sugar, rice, coffee, indigo, and opium. At last they worked their way back to where Miriam and her companions hid, among the crates of chamber pots.

"Here's the Captain!" cried one of the men, striding up to Captain Clooney and knocking him in the head with the lantern in his fist.

"Name your ransom price," Goh Cheng Cheng said, "to let the ship and her cargo and crew pass, and I shall pay it."

The pirate sprang on Goh Cheng Cheng with fists and feet, knocking the older man to the deck. Miriam and Captain Clooney shrank back.

"Enough of that!"

A tall man of commanding air, bent over in the enclosed space, issued the order.

"You never know which ones will bring the best ransom," the tall man said.

"Yes, *Khun*."

"Or which will interest the Golden Dragon." The *khun*, or chief, paused and ran his eye over Miriam in a chilling, appraising way. "Bring them on deck with the others. Get started on this cargo without delay."

Miriam went over to where Goh Cheng Cheng was rising, supporting himself against a barrel. She gave him her shoulder to lean on as the captives made their way through the hold to the ladders.

On deck Miriam, the seamen who'd survived the night, Captain Clooney, and Goh Cheng Cheng, remained shivering all night. They were surrounded by three large junks and a dense fog covering the calm—but oh! nowhere near peaceful sea. Throughout the night, during which the pirates worked steadily to relieve *Caldera* of the merchandize in her hold, cursing and the sound of fists broke out among the men of the junks. They would occasionally leave off their labors to brutalize one of the crew, Captain Clooney, or Goh Cheng Cheng, with the flat of their fearsome *kris*. They seemed to be under orders not to beat Miriam, but periodically her cap or outer garments were pulled and tweaked.

Miriam shuddered at each touch. No one was more aware than she how much gender is a performance. She knew her men's clothes didn't fool the *khun* of the pirates, or any of them, because she chose not to change the way she walked, her mannerisms, her distinctly feminine carriage. On deck Miriam stayed near Captain Clooney and Goh Cheng Cheng, rather than try to blend in with the seamen as a ship's boy should do.

She both feared and longed for the coming of day. Dawn broke and showed the deck of *Caldera* strewn with tea, coffee, sugar, and broken glass from the skylight the pirates crashed through during their excesses of the night. Peering over the ship's side Miriam observed the junks grappled to *Caldera*. Men were filling large open stowage compartments on the junks' decks with Goh Cheng Cheng's cargo. At the same time a homely scene was taking place on the decks of the pirate craft—the cooking of breakfast, women and children, and even dogs and poultry gamboling about.

The sight of the pirates' families struck Miriam oddly. Even robbery, assault and battery, could be a family business. When the mists began to lift with the advancing day, a great hue and cry arose from everyone aboard the junks. Coming at them at speed was a fleet of a dozen more pirate ships.

The *khun* threw down his bowl of rice porridge and pelted across to *Caldera*, cuffing and calling to his men as he came. He ran up and shouted in Captain Clooney's face.

"He says, put this ship in motion," Goh Cheng Cheng translated for the captain. "Sail this ship and follow him to those leeward islands, as you value your life!"

Shaking and trying to wet his parched lips, Captain Clooney stood up.

"None of the men had anything to eat or drink," Miriam said to Goh Cheng Cheng. "Make them give the sailors rice and water, and then they may sail the ship."

Goh Cheng Cheng turned to the *khun*, who cut him off with a wave of his hand. "I understood the *farang*, what do you take me for?"

The pirate captain eyed Miriam, a long considering stare, and shouted orders in harsh tones to his ship. Immediately a large pot of rice and one of tea was handed across. The sailors, Captain Clooney, and Goh Cheng Cheng, crowded in on the food. Miriam was stepping forward to claim her share, when her arm was gripped by the *khun*.

"Now you will learn how your kindness is answered, foreign devil." The man hissed in Miriam's ear. "Cry out if you want to see them die."

The *khun* pulled her toward the stern of the ship. The last bundles of merchandize were being tossed aboard the pirate craft, no longer grappled to *Caldera*, before they made their escape. He pointed over the side at *Caldera's* jolly boat.

"Into the boat, we are taking it too," the *khun* said. "No shouts, no calls."

From the stern of the boat, with the tall, brown, muscular *khun* sitting beside her on the thwart, Miriam watched the scene aboard *Caldera*. Captain Clooney and Goh Cheng Cheng, having once raised their heads from the trough, realized

Miriam was not among them and raced for the lee rail. Goh Cheng Cheng was leaning over the bulwark, raising his clasped hands toward the boat and shouting, "No! Take me, take me!"

Poltroon was the word that rose to Miriam's mind when Captain Clooney, seeing the boat at an irrevocable distance, came forward and added his pleas in a much louder voice than the poor abused supercargo.

"No!" Miriam screamed back.

Thrax was suddenly up on the lee rail, pacing forward and aft with rapid flicks of its tail at every turn. Its head was turned toward the water, concentrating on the surface.

"No!" Miriam cried again. "Oh stay!"

At that instant Thrax leapt overboard, went underwater, and came up stroking toward the jolly boat.

The boat was nearing the *khun's* ship. Miriam's heart pounded to see Thrax pursuing her across the divide, its delicate limbs pumping away under water.

"Go back! Oh!"

Miriam was crying in earnest, for the *khun* ordered the oars shipped to allow Thrax to come closer. Within reach of the boat Thrax raised its upper half above the surface, kicking wildly with its hind quarters. Bobbing its head, Thrax looked for a landing spot within the boat.

At an order from the *khun* an oar came thwacking down, aimed at Thrax's skull. Miriam screamed. Thrax dove and surfaced next alongside the boat's quarter. Weaving there in the water like an ancient sea creature, Thrax's yellow eyes locked on Miriam. Another oar came down and Miriam heard a decided conk.

"No! My God, no! Thraaaax!"

Thrax went under and did not come up again. Tears blinded Miriam in the confusion that followed. The *khun* and his men in the boat were laughing in triumph over the cat. She was pushed up the side of the junk. The *khun* gave her into the charge of one of his women, who led her amidships to where the cargo was stowed. Before she was invited to get down into a stowage compartment, the woman handed Miriam a bowl of rice porridge and a bowl of tea.

"Safer for you." The woman made a motion with her head that Miriam should step down, and then threw a meaning glance in the direction of the dozen junks coming up with a press of sail.

Sniffling and blubbering, and balancing the two bowls, Miriam climbed down into a rectangular wood box set into the deck of the vessel. The woman gave Miriam a pitying look before she and a companion fixed the lid over the compartment.

One and three quarters of a mile away, a wet and furious creature came up on the beach of the nearest of the atoll for which the pirates were fleeing. Tigers were not unknown on the mainland of that part of the world, but though this cat was the size of a tiger it had a coat the tawny color of the Thracian steppes. It shook sea water from its fur in brisk fashion, and proceeded to sniff about, ending with its muzzle in the air. The Hell-Cat's lips pulled away from its fangs as it concentrated on tasting the wind. Swinging its great head down, it set off with a low snarling growl in the direction of the next islet in the atoll.

CHAPTER TWELVE

Maximus had been dissatisfied and bedeviled ever since Miriam sailed in *Caldera*. On the desk before him in the great cabin were sketches and calculations of the optimum shape and angle of the stunsails during ascent and landing that he'd been working on, to save his sanity. For the last ten minutes, though, Maximus had been writing in a journal. He dipped his pen and began again in the mixture of Gaelic and English he used for this personal diary, to confuse the enemy.

"Saramago tiptoes round me, telling his mates, 'Have a care and no cross the skipper, he fit to 'splode.' I have been angry, damnably hipped, snappish, and frustrated, but it is with my own weakness. I should have prevented that dear woman from throwing herself in the way of danger, whatever it might have cost me in loss of her esteem. The truth is I was afraid to displease her. I only said she should go to live with my relations—my relations!—because I thought it was what she wanted to hear, nay needed to hear, for the sake of honour. Instead disappointment filled that lovely face, and how I have repented those words! Each hour and day that passes increases my grief and regret, for what might be happening to her, for not using the time I had with her in Hong Kong to better purpose. Do I deceive myself? Can it really be that dearest of women wants to live with me—and this motley crew of mine —aboard a crack ship?"

Saramago slid into the great cabin, and at sight of his steward's eager face Maximus leaped up so forcefully he knocked over the desk chair.

"*El capitán Americano*, your honor," Saramago said, righting the chair. "The watch say it's the Flincher, Sir, put in on native junk."

As soon as Miriam sailed, Maximus caused a watch to be set at the quay. For *Caldera*, or any sight of Captain Clooney or a deputation sent to negotiate ransom.

"Second best hat and coat, Saramago."

"Aye, aye, sir." Saramago knuckled his forehead, turned as though to obey, and stopped. "You no believe who captain de junk as brought the Flincher in, sir."

Maximus pushed past his steward into his sleeping cabin, stowed his private journal, and came out with the uniform jacket and cocked hat under his arm.

Saramago called after Maximus. "That creature el Bora it was, sir!"

Maximus was in a muck sweat by the time he reached the building where the British Consul had his headquarters. Inside the spacious entryway, Maximus pulled his shirt away from his skin and stood for a moment beneath the ceiling fans. A system of belts, wheels, and servants kept the fans in constant motion. Maximus was collecting himself to go in to the Consul when out of Francis Blackwell's private chamber issued Jugma Bora. Seaman Bora stepped out with a swagger and a pleased, self-satisfied smile on his lips.

"You there, hold hard!" Maximus said.

The smug look instantly left Bora's face and he took fright, dashing forward and back, performing a dance with Maximus in the anti-chamber.

"This will nae do, ye great weasel." Maximus punched Bora in the head, then moved round and caught him by the back of the neck on the rebound. "We will be revisiting his honor Mr. Blackwell now, sure."

Maximus burst into the Consul's private office without a knock or by your leave, clutching seaman Bora, whose eyes rolled in his head. Francis Blackwell and Captain Clooney started to their feet.

"What is the meaning of this, sir?" Captain Clooney cried. "Unhand the good Chinese. That man was the only one to speak for us, after the others stripped *Caldera* bare. They took our boats, sir." Captain Clooney appealed to Francis. "Every scrape of canvas. Sheets, lines, and spars, even the rudder. Left us to grind away on our beef bones."

"God damn your beef bones, sir. This is no good Chinese." Maximus gave Jugma Bora a shake. "Allow me to present Jugma Bora, Siamese pirate."

There were exclamations at this, not least from seaman Bora.

"Seaman Bora here was aboard *Nonesuch* at Lord Exmouth's direction," Maximus said to Francis Blackwell. "When the ship was attacked in the Celebes, our good man here tried to turn Miss Albuyeh over to his compatriots."

Francis gave Bora a hard stare. "What have you to say to that? After you took this man's reward into the bargain."

"He mistake me," Jugma Bora said. "I no the man. We all look alike to the *farang*."

"Oh, aye?" Maximus said. "To a China-man that would be *júwàirén*. You taught us that." Done with these preliminaries Maximus yanked up Jugma Bora's tunic. "And how will ye be explaining my boot mark on your chest?"

That capped it for Francis, he shouted for the Sergeant of Marines.

"Give me a moment with the prisoner, Mr. Blackwell, I beg." Maximus shook Jugma Bora, he'd not let go of him for an instant. "I will know where they will be taking her, do you hear me there?"

"And I will have the twenty-five reales I gave you returned," Captain Clooney put in.

Such fury rose to Maximus's eyes that Captain Clooney backed away.

"That was ill-timed," the American captain said. "I beg your pardon."

The door was opened by a marine, and Admiral Hoste, the senior naval officer on station, walked into the room followed by a uniformed entourage.

"Where is she, Bora, and I shall intercede for you," Maximus said, with a final rattle. "You know her generous nature, she would want me to do that much. Otherwise I shall let them hang you for a pirate today itself."

The lid the women placed over the compartment Miriam was in had a slot running round its edge that allowed in air and light, for the benefit of poultry and other livestock that Miriam could smell and hear round her. They were alike, kept aboard in their pens. The space was so small Miriam couldn't sit upright, much less stand, and she either had to lean over hugging her legs or lie prone on the wood deck. By contorting this way and that, Miriam was able to catch glimpses of sky, sea, and the working of the vessel.

She was so blinded by tears and grief for Thrax when they'd first imprisoned her, Miriam had no clear recollection of what happened just after she came aboard the pirate ship. There had been a great noise of hurrying feet and shouted cries. The *khun's* ship hadn't lingered to parlay with the next wave of marauders. When she grew calmer Miriam began to wonder when she'd be released, since the danger to her captors of having their prizes snatched away was past.

The day waned, the rhythm of the ship changed, as though lying to for the night, and Miriam remained bowed over. Her fear and desperation increased as the light died. Miriam heard the clucking protests of a bird separated from its brethren, then sounds of butchery, followed by the happy ones of supper preparing—women's voices and the laughter of children. Miriam's stomach rumbled when the smells of cooking reached her, and then she screamed.

It was full dark, at least in Miriam's prison, and something had run over her feet. She became aware there were many scurrying, crawling creatures sharing the compartment with her. Another scream, unnatural sounding, was torn from her throat.

It brought a boy and girl, running to peer in at her. They looked like blessed angels to Miriam. She spoke to them in Malay. "Dears, let me out. There are...vermin in here."

The angels laughed. "It is only rats and spiders, and the spiders are good to eat."

Miriam shuddered, her gorge rising. The *khun* shouted the children away, and the lid was lifted from over Miriam's head. In spite of cramped muscles, fear and revulsion drove Miriam to spring forth on the deck like a cat. The people of the junk found this funny too. Looking down into the compartment Miriam saw velvety fat bodied spiders moving about, wood lice, and the tails of rats as they squeezed themselves into the adjoining compartments to avoid the lantern light.

"See Miss, see!" the little girl trapped a spider by laying a small stick exactly between head and thorax. She picked it up and extended the spider for Miriam to inspect, her small fingers between its thick legs.

"Oh yes, well done," Miriam said, stomach roiling and skin crawling.

Not to be outdone, the little boy waved the spider he trapped at her, and cried, "And then all you do is—" and he skewered his spider onto the stick he'd caught it with.

The children scampered off with their snacks to the galley. Miriam was not unaware the *khun* had been watching her closely during this interlude. She thought about the knife in her boot, she would resist going back in that hole.

"Come with me," the *khun's* voice came out of the night. "There is someone you should meet."

He led Miriam to the galley, where more children and three women were chatting and stirring pots of delicious smelling food. Miriam's stomach protested audibly in the silence, when the little group turned to look her over. Her hopes were rising she would be given something to eat, treated decently, and not forced back into a verminous pit.

"Here she is," the *khun* announced.

The women's gazes were stern. The eldest among them stepped forward and slapped Miriam's face. Miriam swayed back, surprised more than anything; the woman hadn't struck her hard.

"You're the one! The British spy."

Miriam said nothing, but gazed steadily back at the older woman, trying to keep a neutral expression of face.

"Because of you, the Golden Dragon took a daughter from each of the Boat People. Made us keen to find you, whoever laid hold of you could have their own back. And because of you, Captain," the woman raised her voice to the *khun*, standing at the head of his men, "it will be my daughter who is returned in exchange for this foreign devil."

There was a general cry of happy agreement. Miriam felt gut punched. The Golden Dragon was no ship.

Miriam sucked in a great breath. "I don't know anything of dragons or devils or British," she said. "I'm a merchant's daughter, from Iran."

The woman looked at Miriam like she'd spoken Greek.

"Little Dragon says differently," the *khun* put in mildly.

Oh, that bastard Bora!

"Please don't put me back in that hole." Miriam appealed to the woman. "I won't run away, I can't. In the morning I will go quietly and take the place of your girl."

"You will long for the spiders and rats when the Golden Dragon has you."

That hurt Miriam far more than the slap earlier.

"See here, Mai," the *khun* said in a reasoning tone, "the white woman can't say fairer than that. And you won't think of casting yourself overboard." The *khun* turned to Miriam. "Because there are snakes in these waters, deadly poisonous ones. That's why the place works so well as a prison island for the Golden Dragon. Less men needed for guards."

Miriam's eyes filled with tears, she couldn't help it, and the woman Mai came right up close to her. She thought she would receive another slap. Instead Mai patted Miriam's cheeks with both hands and led her to a seat in the galley, and a bowl of rice and stewed fowl.

Miriam ate the meal, though at the end she had to force down the slightly raw flesh of the bird so as not to offend the Boat People. She tried desperately to enjoy sitting upright near the galley stove with the women, listening to the pops and hisses as the children roasted their spiders on sticks. But the women's talk turned to the nephew the Golden Dragon had taken for a lover. Miriam could think of little else; a prison island, and the Golden Dragon not a ship. It was something or someone willing to torture its own people. Greed, revenge, lust, what vices drove this Dragon, Miriam couldn't guess—not from the perspective of her sheltered upbringing. She told herself she must be grateful for these moments of peace, and relative freedom, in the cool night air.

Mai glanced over at her as the sound of the men dicing nearby in the ship became louder, and Miriam knew that freedom was at an end.

"Safer for you back there."

Legs trembling, Miriam followed Mai to the stowage area. She asked for the privy on the way and Mai took her to the seat of ease, and stood patiently by while Miriam used it and washed from a bucket of water left there for the purpose. Being clean put some heart into Miriam.

"Leave me a lantern, I beg," Miriam said, glimpsing the vermin slithering in the hole.

Mai glared at her. "Yes, alright, you get in."

Miriam stepped gingerly into the stowage compartment. She took off her jacket and tented it over her head, reaching out for the lantern. Mai handed it down to her, and beckoned for one of the other women to assist her with the lid.

"My advice to you, put out the candle if you hear the men coming. You do not want the light to attract them after they've been drinking *cava*."

Better rats and spiders than that, Miriam agreed. She crouched down with the lantern between her boots, while the lid, alive with crawling things, was fixed over her head. Miriam pulled the jacket tight round her, and hovered over the light.

She was practically in a coffin, where her Mama and everyone throughout her girlhood told Miriam she would end if she didn't do what she was told. If she left home and ventured out alone to try to make a life for herself. She'd been an impressionable girl then, now her woman's heart ached for Thrax and her own predicament.

Miriam sat hugging her knees, crying and rocking a little over her lantern, and then she heard men's voices. The voices came nearer and Miriam, her hand shaking, lifted the lantern and blew out the candle with a wet breath. She steeled herself in the darkness against the onslaught of little clawed feet.

The men went round the ship snugging all down for the night. Miriam felt the first furry bodies brush against her hands and run over her feet, and stifled a cry with an effort. Determined to make an even greater one, Miriam laid her head on her knees and turned her mind away.

She started by reciting the *shahadah*, the Muslim profession of faith. *There is no god but God, and Mohammed is His Messenger.* And then recalled the Apostle's Creed of the

Christians, that she'd learned from Francis Blackwell. *I believe in God the Father Almighty, maker of heaven and earth.* She reached back in memory for every detail, every moment, of that last ascent and descent in *Nonesuch*, when Captain Thorpe allowed her to remain on deck. The glory of it, the vast star filled night sky. The feeling at once of limitless freedom, and of belonging to the community of the ship.

> This house is resplendent and joyous to-night
> The beautiful lamps give a dazzling light:
> Oh this night! This night, it is fit to inspire
> Every heart with the passion of love and desire

Persian verses ran through her mind, comforting her with their timeless beauty and imagery. Miriam wished she'd seized more of life in Hong Kong, she regretted keeping Captain Thorpe at a distance. She must find the courage to survive no matter what occurred in order to be part of that world again, to experience the sensation of being alive in every fibre when the ship *Nonesuch* was in the ether, where she could reach out her hand and a brave man would take it.

CHAPTER THIRTEEN

In the morning when the lid was lifted, Miriam lay like a dead woman stretched full length on the deck. Mai gave a shriek of despair and jumped down into the compartment. During the early hours just after dawn, the spiders and rats having melted away to their daytime abodes, Miriam stretched out prone in exhaustion. When Mai landed beside her, Miriam woke with a start, a deck seam etched across her face.

Over a breakfast of rice porridge and tea, the *khun* announced that the exchange of captives had been arranged with the prison island. The pirate vessel rocked gently on the placid swell, while bright rays of morning sunshine made the mists rise from the sea in delicate upward spirals. After the meal—her share of porridge with egg Miriam barely and with difficulty ate—she was taken to the lee side of the junk and invited down into *Caldera's* jolly boat.

"This time of year," Mai whispered to her, before Miriam went over the side, "no snakes in these waters."

The junk lay close to the island during the night. The prison island was one of a series or atoll, like chucks of mountainous jungle thrown down by handfuls into the sea. Miriam could swim the distance to the strand the jolly boat pulled toward, it wasn't far. She shivered in spite of the humidity of the morning.

The jolly boat ground ashore, and the *khun* took Miriam's arm to assist her out of the boat. She stepped into ankle deep water, shimmering, warm, and iridescent. Miriam was marched up the beach surrounded by the *khun* and his men toward a dense ring of vegetation. A trail running into the jungle came into view, and four men stepped from under cover of the trees.

Miriam and all on her side halted. The four men, heavily muscled, tattooed and scarred, had with them a girl of no more than thirteen. The girl cried out when she saw the *khun* and his men, and received a vigorous shake for it from the man holding her bound wrists. Miriam tried to meet the girl's eyes but found her gaze avoided, Mai's daughter was crying too hard at sight of her rescuers. At least Miriam's hands were not tied, though her heart was constricted and heavy inside her chest.

By some signal Miriam did not detect, she and the girl were pushed roughly forward at the same instant. The *khun* caught the sobbing girl, and one of the black-toothed guards kept Miriam from falling down. She recovered her footing at once and stepped away from them. The Dragon's men laughed.

"What are you waiting for? Bugger off."

The *khun* picked the girl up in his arms, and he and his men double-timed it to the jolly boat.

The four men surrounding Miriam turned back up the footpath. She went along with them and kept their pace, not wanting to give cause for them to bind her hands, or indeed to handle her in any way. These were very rough men, with their blackened teeth and their hair done up in top knots—warrior fashion. Miriam doubted they were Muslim or Christian, or anything anyone had ever heard of.

When the footpath opened on to a cluster of thatched huts Miriam felt her legs go weak, especially as the men began to purposely shoulder and touch her. A woman's voice floated out from a hut as they passed, a simple tune like a lullaby, incongruous in their surroundings. It was sung in some European language. German? Or Dutch. Miriam stared sharply round toward the sound.

"No, Missy," one of the men said, mistaking why Miriam turned away, "take a good look."

In the center of the ring of huts was a stock for imprisoning the head and hands. Miriam recoiled. It was stained rust colored like the whipping posts and triangles of Harriman's Hole. Mixed in with the churned mud beneath the stocks was blood, and worse.

"That's where the Golden Dragon puts girls who try to escape."

Miriam gasped, fighting down full panic, fearing any moment she'd be forced into one of the huts, alone with the four men.

At one end of the circle was the largest hut, and the men shoved Miriam toward it. They pinched and squeezed her as they neared it. Miriam choked back her sobs, her fingers tingling toward the handle of the *sgian dubh*. She had no illusions about battling the four guards, but with the knowledge from Maximus's tutelage, Miriam thought she might be able to effectively stab herself.

She stumbled inside the hut, and came face to face with the smallest Chinese woman in all creation. Her relief at seeing another woman was so great, Miriam sobbed aloud.

"What are you about?" the little woman shrieked at the four men. "Haven't I told you not to mishandle them? Get out! Don't go far."

The four thugs bowled one another over in their haste to get away through the door opening carved in the thatch.

Miriam heard the men take up positions outside. The little woman, meanwhile, was climbing up and taking a seat in an ornate wooden chair set atop a low table.

When she could look down on Miriam from this eminence, her bony fingers clutching the gilded chair arms carved to resemble the heads of open mouthed dragons, the small woman flashed Miriam a yellow toothed grimace.

"I shall call them back in a trice if you displease me. Understand? Don't speak!"

Miriam nodded, closing her mouth and casting her gaze deferentially down.

"I'll give you permission when you may speak. My nephew told me of your coming here, to My dominions. He said you were promising. A girl with spirit, a likely girl awake on every suit, resourceful and knowing, and that is just what I need at present. Are you such a one, girl, are you...promising?"

The woman gave Miriam a regal inclination of her head.

"Yes," Miriam squeaked out. The memory of a luminous bow wave and Jugma Bora's talk of heirs and empires came to her. "I speak five languages and—" the woman slammed an open palm down on the top of a dragon's head. Miriam hastened to say, "What would you require of such a promising person?"

"Ah! Better, you understand you are here to serve Me. What is it I require? Information and retribution. I want to know the movements of ships—my own number in the thousands. Warships from China, Britain, and Holland come to annoy me, and I should like to be ready for them."

The little woman leaned back in her throne-like chair staring at Miriam, rubbing the dragon heads and grunting.

"What would you do?" she shrilled of a sudden. "To evade the attentions of those men outside, not to die screaming?"

"Whatever you wish," Miriam stammered.

"Good answer." The woman leaned forward, her feet dangling short of the table below. "All you need do to avoid such a fate is—two things." She paused and bared teeth in shades of amber and brown, while Miriam held her breath. "First, you will summon the ship that brought you here. I will have an airship, and that will take care of my information needs."

Miriam's heart raced. Lure Captain Thorpe and his ship into a trap? She might be able to warn him off before he fell into it. Through the open doorway of the hut, Miriam caught glimpses of the leering faces and sweating bodies of the Dragon's men. This was her reality, those rough men. What would she do to escape it, could she act the betrayer to those who'd been kindest to her?

The diminutive Chinese woman pushed up out of her chair to stand on the low table, leaning over Miriam. "Second, there must be retribution for you coming here without My leave. Someone must be punished. You shall prove your intentions to serve Me by selecting a girl from among my captives to satisfy the lusts of my men."

"No." Miriam answered instantly. "I won't do it."

The Chinese woman stumbled down off the table and struck Miriam twice, *slap slap*, much more fiercely than Mai had done. She wore large rings on her baby hands, which hurt amazingly. Miriam's vision cleared but she kept her head bowed.

The woman swayed on tiny feet before her, and the shrill voice demanded, "Do you know who I am? What I am?"

"The Boat People spoke of a dragon," Miriam said.

"Did I say you could speak?" She dealt Miriam another pair of raps. "The Golden Dragon. You know my name. There is nothing and no one that is traded, sold, ransomed, outraged, or murdered in these Seas that does not pass through Me. Hence the Golden. Say it!"

"Golden Dragon," Miriam said. "You are the Golden Dragon."

"And you are the British spy."

"I'm a merchant's daughter from Iran." Miriam had appropriated her mother's history, and she meant to stick to it.

This time the Golden Dragon balled a little fist and hit Miriam in the breast. Miriam drew back, hugging her chest, her mouth open in shock.

"You are what I say you are! How dare you say no to Me!" The Golden Dragon sucked in a breath, swaying on feet Miriam took to be deformed they were so small. The woman murmured to herself, "Little Dragon was taken in. I gave her the power, and she refused it. They should take who can! A pretty face and white teeth alone will never be My heir."

The Dragon gave Miriam a malevolent glare with eyes so dark the pupils were hard to distinguish, like an animal's. "Weak, foolish girl! You should have accepted my conditions. What I offer, you must accept! Over there."

She pointed to a corner of the hut. Miriam moved with relief to be out of direct sight of the guards. That area of the hut was furnished with two rush chairs, one missing the woven seat, and a sideboard or chest of drawers. Atop the sideboard was an array of edged weapons, and evil looking instruments that chilled Miriam to her soul. In a carved sandalwood box open on the sideboard was a jadeite or stone—

"Take off your boots!" The Golden Dragon ordered. "Start with the one with the knife! You cannot fool the Dragon, Missy. I can see you think yourself clever."

The Golden Dragon's arm shot out to strike her, but Miriam sat down on the whole chair and tugged at the boot. She could easily unbalance the Dragon, on her limiting little knobs of feet. *Slip the knife out, and straight into the throat.* During practice with Captain Thorpe her hands never shook this much, and there weren't four guards eager to pounce on her within shouting distance. The boot and her knife were snatched from Miriam's shaking hands before they were off her foot.

"You are going to tell me who sent you and why. How to signal that airship and all about those British dogs, the greatest pirates in the world." The Golden Dragon waved a bejeweled hand at her. "Off with the rest of it!"

"No."

Miriam was hauled to her feet by the preternaturally strong Dragon. A very ill breath said in her face, "Strip, or I shall have my men tear the clothes from your body. They will enjoy that."

With trembling hands and a quivering lower lip she couldn't control, Miriam removed her jacket, gown, scarves, trowsers, and small clothes.

"How much clothing does one scrawny girl need?" The Dragon complained halfway through Miriam's disrobing.

Miriam stood shivering, trying to cover her nakedness with her arms, one boot her only remaining clothing. The Dragon took no notice of it.

"Sit down there. I'm going to lash you to the chair. It's easier that way."

Indicating the bottomless chair with a jerk of her head, the Dragon took up a long length of twisted cord. Fear rooted her to the spot, Miriam couldn't move to the chair.

The Dragon jumped on her. "Do you know what I do with a girl who won't cooperate? I put her in the stocks without a stitch on and let the guards have her."

Miriam sobbed and sat as well as she could with her legs apart, balanced on the chair frame. The Golden Dragon made a quick job of tying Miriam by wrists and ankles to the chair.

"Let's start, shall we?" The Dragon took up a *parang* from the sideboard, and returned waiving it in Miriam's face. "Who sent you, British whore?"

"My...my father is a merchant in Iran, a wealthy man. If it is ransom you want—"

Miriam teetered on her chair when the Dragon struck her with the wood handle of the knife.

"I won't spoil your beauty, I never do. You will fetch a high price for me, after I get what I want."

The Dragon stood considering the implements on the sideboard. It felt a horrible long time for Miriam waiting there, straining against the cords binding her. A million thoughts raced through her mind, terror only just kept below the surface.

When the Dragon turned round with the jadeite phallus huge in her tiny hand, Miriam blurted out, "I'll tell you everything!"

"Yes, you will."

The Golden Dragon came swiftly up to Miriam and whacked her in the chest. Miriam fell backward, her head rebounding against the dirt floor. She cried out, shaking, strapped to a bottomless chair. The Dragon loomed closer. Not like this! Her first time must not be an act of brutality, of dominance and power. Why had she been reticent with that good man Maximus Thorpe, and missed the chance for tenderness and love? Miriam heard voices in her head repeating the same phrases. This was what happened to women who did not obey, who dared leave home without the protection of a man. She screamed, loud and long, a full-throated cry of frustration and rage.

Miriam refused to look away as the Golden Dragon stooped down, aiming that stone monstrosity at her. She jerked hard sideways in the chair when the Dragon's head came level with her raised knees, and felt the satisfying connection of her boot with the Dragon's skull. Surprised shouts, scuffling, and a commotion came from outside the thatched walls. A tawny colored blur flew past Miriam's feet, and landed with a thud against the back wall of the hut.

There was a whoosh as from a deflating balloon, and Miriam turned her head toward the sound. Against the wall of the hut, Thrax was on top of the Golden Dragon. Thrax's eyes cut over to Miriam and its lips raised in salute, the grip of its fangs never loosening from the Dragon's neck. The Hell-Cat emitted a woof like the barking of a tiger.

Miriam screamed, this time in horror, fright, and triumph. She closed her eyes for a second upon it all, then opened them, avoiding the sight of Thrax and the Golden Dragon. Was she going to lie there naked and wait for the surviving men to regain their courage and walk in? Miriam thrashed side to side on the dirt floor until one of the flimsy chair arms gave way, and she was able to free one hand. She untied the rattan cords and rose shakily to her feet, stumbled over and slumped against the sideboard.

The *sgian dubh* and her second boot were heaped together and Miriam stooped to put them on. She had to brave the sight of Thrax tearing the throat out of the Golden Dragon, because her clothes were carried away by the Hell-Cat's rush and lay in a heap at the back of the hut. Thrax growled at her as she neared on tiptoe. Tiger-like when it rescued her from the Dragon, the Hell-Cat was now the size of a lesser cousin, a panther or mountain lion.

"Ugh!" Miriam couldn't help an exclamation of disgust, for Thrax began to purr, spewing blood sideways from its jaws. "I shall not interfere with you," she hastened to assure it, "not in the least."

The bodice of her gown was heavy with gouts of blood, but Miriam donned it and the other splattered garments as fast as she could. Fully dressed, she stepped back to the sideboard, and selected a belt with a *parang* in a wooden sheath and strapped it round her waist. She'd just taken a vicious straight blade *kris* in her hand when a guard poked his head into the hut. The man screamed, making Miriam jump. His eyes rolled up in his head, and he staggered away shrieking.

"Thrax! Thrax, do you hear me there?" Miriam tried to put the note of command in her voice she'd heard the Navy men use. "I go in search of the ladies, and when I come away I expect you to leave off this business and attend me." Miriam turned away from Thrax.

The gore and savagery of the Golden Dragon's life had been visited on her in the manner of her death. Miriam slipped out the back of the hut, gripping the intricately patterned *kris* and feeling primed to use it if she encountered any guards.

Behind the ring of huts Miriam discovered paths leading to the privies. She skirted their reek and followed the sound of singing. It amazed her that somehow, after what happened, there could still be lullabies and a woman's sweet voice in the world.

Miriam stepped inside one of the huts and found a collection of women, a few sitting against the thatched walls while others reclined on pallets. None of them looked her way or took particular notice of her entrance. An old ayah or servant woman squatting on a three-legged stool turned her head with an interested stare, when Miriam passed by *kris* in hand.

The woman who was singing stood out from the rest. She had golden hair and a pert upturned nose, features Miriam remembered from a miniature portrait.

"Anna Lovell? *Parlez-vous francais?*"

"How do you know my name?"

The woman's eyes were unfocused, and then with a visible effort she concentrated on Miriam's face.

"No," the woman said, "I don't know you. You are just another victim of the Dragon."

Anna Lovell waved her hand at the women draped round the hut. They didn't pay Miriam and Anna the least heed, though French was a language seldom heard near the South China Sea.

Miriam eased down beside Anna, putting her back to a thatched wall, so that she faced the way she'd entered. At once Miriam felt someone watching her, and noticed for the first time a woman tied up on the opposite side of the hut. The sight frightened Miriam anew, and she'd barely ceased shuddering from her last experience.

"I am not a victim," Miriam said, through gritted teeth. "Anna, do not cry out. The Golden Dragon is no more. Dead, she...it's dead. And now we are leaving here, all of us."

Anna put her face in her hands and sobbed. Even this didn't draw the attention of the women round them.

"What is wrong with them?" Miriam said. She knew only a fraction of the torture these women might have endured, but Miriam couldn't understand their incredible languor. All except for the fierce looking person hog tied like a beast.

Wiping tears and mucus from her face, Anna said, "Opium. The Dragon, the guards, give them opium in the morning. Keeps them quiet."

Miriam absorbed the shock of this additional violation. She found Anna surprisingly alert, but didn't want to take notice of it and distress her. "Anna, can you help me with them? We are all leaving, every one."

To encourage her Miriam stood, gave Anna her hand, and hauled her to her feet. Miriam hefted the *kris* in her hand.

"Oh no, Mademoiselle!" Anna Lovell cried, when Miriam made toward the woman bound across the hut. "Not the Hottentot! She is a mad woman, she used to be a guard here. She will kill us all if you let her loose."

Miriam had a flash of comprehension that made her feel ill. *Do you know what I do with a girl who won't cooperate?*

"You would be mad too," Miriam said. "If you were the one being tortured to terrify the rest."

Those words were braver than Miriam felt as she went across the hut, to the woman tied by wrists and ankles with rattan cord that looped also round her neck. She was covered in smuts, wearing a ragged pair of the petticoat bloomers common among the Chinese, and a tunic ripped off one shoulder so the fact she was missing a breast was exposed. An old wound, well healed, but fearful nonetheless. As Miriam neared she could smell her, the woman's legs were stained with blood and filth.

Wobbling slightly, Miriam knelt in front of the woman.

"*Salaam alay-kum*," the black woman said, when they faced one another.

Miriam was so astonished she plopped down hard on her butt. "*Walay kum-salaam.*" And to you, peace.

"Give me sacred *kris*, *khun*," the woman said. "Set me free, and you have no need to fear guards."

"I was worried about them," Miriam said. "I shall certainly release you."

Miriam purposefully sheathed the *kris*, and pulling out the *parang* she cut the cord binding the woman. They rose unsteadily together, Miriam trying to hold the other woman's eye.

"The Golden Dragon is dead," Miriam said.

"You kill her, *khun*? Those your screams earlier?"

"Yes." Miriam wouldn't be humble and lower her gaze, when facing a ferocious creature it was best not to look away. "That was before, now the Dragon's dead, and I'm taking these women away. Are there more in the other huts?"

"Huts full of plunder, this one only with human cargo. This side of island, other side is men's prison."

God have mercy, Miriam thought. "How—" she stammered, "how many guards are there here?"

"Six."

Thrax may have accounted for one or more of the four who escorted Miriam in, but that left more than enough to recapture these drugged souls. With a thudding heart she removed the belt with *kris* and *parang* from round her waist. Miriam knew she was no warrior, she heard Anna Lovell cry out as she handed the weapons over to a woman that was one.

"Come back here immediately after," Miriam said. The woman took the belt from her with an expression like the one she'd seen on Maximus Thorpe's face before battle. "I will rouse these poor creatures, and be ready to leave as soon as you return."

"You wear it wrong," the woman said, adjusting the belt over one shoulder so that it covered her missing breast.

She was not much taller than Miriam, but every ounce of the woman seemed made of muscle and coiled power. She drew the *kris* and flexed her fingers round the curved bone hilt, adjusting her grip.

Before the black woman left the hut, looking like one of the furies of hell, she paused for a moment near Anna Lovell. "Ask her why she not drunk on opium like the rest," she called over her shoulder to Miriam. What sounded like a growl escaped her, Anna recoiled, and the woman strode out of the hut.

"You will never see her more," Anna Lovell said in a critical tone, coming up to Miriam. "And God help you if she returns to her old ways and unites with the guards against us."

"I doubt that will happen," Miriam said.

Inwardly Miriam thought, *Basmallah!* In the name of God, the Compassionate, the Merciful, let it not be true that she'd armed an enemy.

CHAPTER FOURTEEN

The black woman returned with her sword arm red to the elbow. She went over to a bucket near the old ayah and washed the blood matter-of-factly from her arm and the *kris*. Miriam, by a miracle, had all the ladies standing and clutching a long length of twisted cord.

"No more guards to worry you, *khun*." The black woman placed her palms together and made a bow, her weapons clean and slung across her body once more.

Miriam bowed in acknowledgement, hiding the sick feeling she had at heart for ordering the deaths of fellow men. "Do you know this island? I need to find a headland, to signal for a ship." She would not call her by name, nor say *my ship*, but how her hopes turned upon *Nonesuch* and her people. "Not in the direction of any other settlement on the island," Miriam added, to be clear.

"If this lot handle a short swim," the woman said, "we go across to Dragon's Claw. Next spit of land over."

She'd heard all she cared to of dragons, but Miriam nodded her head. "You lead us."

She held up the end of the line that she was tied to. In front of her Miriam had placed Anna Lovell, who stood giving her back to Miriam's conversation with the Hottentot.

Anna tensed visibly as the black woman withdrew the *kris* from its carved wood and metal sheath, looped to her belt, and offered it to Miriam.

"No, you keep it, you...know best how to use it. I have a weapon." Miriam thought of Thrax, but she raised her trowser leg to show the dagger in her boot.

A flash of white teeth in a brief smile lit the woman's face. "I never laugh at you, *Khun*, after what you did to the Dragon." A shake of her head and an introspective look told Miriam she'd seen the Golden Dragon's torn body. "Call out if you see or hear anyone, and I be with you."

The woman stalked off to the front of the column, tied the cord about her waist and cried, "Ho!"

The line of women, a dozen strong, some tied to and others clutching the line keeping them together, moved out through the back entrance of the hut. The only one left was the old ayah still sitting on the three-legged stool. When Miriam was abreast of her, she called a halt.

"Can you walk?" Miriam asked.

"Watch me."

The old woman pushed to her feet and Miriam placed her in line before her.

"Now we are thirteen," Anna grumbled, turning round, "an unfavorable number."

"Shut it, Missy," the old woman said in Malay. "I had enough of your shit."

"She says don't be superstitious." Miriam translated for Anna Lovell, and the line moved off.

Passing by the largest hut, the group of women gave it a wide berth. Besides the horrid recollections of what happened there to all of them, there was a funky smell emanating from the place and a tremendous noise of busy flies.

"Thrax!" Miriam called in English. "Thrax, to me!"

The black woman, Anna, and the old ayah, the alertest among them, turned and stared at Miriam as though she'd been barking like a dog. Miriam was alone in looking back as they left the ring of huts, to see the Hell-Cat dash from the Golden

Dragon's lair and disappear into the jungle. As she entered the dense forest behind the black woman hacking her way into it, Miriam breathed a sigh of relief. Their flank was covered.

The old ayah, Nguyen Lan from Penang, turned out to be the bravest traveler among them barring the black woman. She went stolidly along on her wide peasant feet, moving ahead in the column to help a woman who'd gone face first up a mud embankment, or slipped in a stream, then return without comment to take her place in line. On the easier parts of the trek she told Miriam her account of being taken captive by pirates, traded from ship captain to ship captain, until ending up years later in the Golden Dragon's clutches. Having reached a certain age by that time, Lan was set to tending the young marketable slaves of the Dragon. "Hauling in water, and hauling out shit," was how Lan put it. Miriam better understood Lan's earlier remark to Anna Lovell.

The place between islands where they were to swim across was weighing on Miriam's mind by the time the party of women emerged from the jungle onto a beach. She didn't know how many were swimmers, and if they could keep together during a crossing. The line of women straggling across the beach to the waters edge was moving with a livelier step, most of the women conscious now of their surroundings. They looked around as though wondering how they'd got there, but each and every one of them maintained a death grip on the cord like a lifeline.

"I'll go find out where we are to cross," Miriam said to Lan, untying the line from her waist. "What is her name?"

"The feral one?" Lan said. "Who knows."

"Sit down, rest a minute," Miriam said in three different languages as she made her way up the line.

"I hope we may get them up again." Miriam confided to the black woman, who was covered in sweat and massaging her machete arm.

"No worries there, *Khun*. Tell them guards on our tail, see how fast they move. Merciful God knows we left a clear track to follow."

Miriam glanced back at the place where they'd come out of the jungle, hoping Thrax was there. But wasn't it just as likely the Hell-Cat would run off on its own wild capers, or return to partake of more of its kill?

"How likely is pursuit?" Miriam shuddered, asking this. "Do the guards from the men's prison come to the women's side?"

"Oh, they come, guards vie to work with women. Brutality and violations, same in both camps. Pursuit? Depends when men's side guards come, maybe few days."

The exit strategy must function splendidly in every particular.

Miriam's anxiety was palpable and the black woman said, in a tone of reassurance, "Even if guards come early, *Khun*, they pagan, superstitious. Once they see what happened to Golden Dragon, her favored men, I misdoubt they have courage to follow. Though the path led to gates of paradise."

"Very well," Miriam said, trying to sound cheered. "Where do we cross? *I* misdoubt all these women can swim."

"Those can, Boat People children." The woman gestured toward a cluster of eight girls and young woman. "You?" Miriam nodded yes. "And me. That leaves ayah Lan, Bengali lady, and the fat *farang*. The golden haired ungrateful one."

Miriam felt that was a little harsh. "She cannot help the way she was born."

"I tire of that excuse." The black woman rose from where she was crouched down, resting. "This way, I show you where."

In the end the black woman swam across with the eight capable young women and left them in a knot on the far bank clutching the twisted cord between them, while she went back to help Miriam with the rest. One by one, they ferried the other women across. It was not difficult for there was but a short swim and the rest was accomplished walking in chest deep water, with Miriam on one side and the black warrior on the other.

At last they were all together on the opposite bank. Miriam was near spent from the day's sufferings and exertions, and hoped they'd not much farther to go. The black woman arranged them in line again, patting a cheek here and there, not viciously but to enliven them, and tied the end about Miriam's waist.

"You said headland, *Khun*, that means uphill. No stopping, we reach a prime spot by nightfall."

Twilight, and the women arrived at the headland stumbling with fatigue. They gained the summit of a horseshoe shaped outcropping of limestone rock, leaning over the sea. The jungle had a lesser hold here, and on three sides sheer cliffs fell away to the beach below. Pursuit could only come from the direction of the jungle.

"Prime, indeed," Miriam said to their guide.

The women were settling down among strewn boulders.

"It gets better."

The black woman led Miriam to the edge of the cliff. In the fading light the woman pointed out the head of a trail winding down to a secluded cove. A path inaccessible except from the spot they occupied. Miriam and the warrior woman shared a satisfied smile.

"I should like to lie down and have a caulk, as the mariners say." Miriam was light-headed from the long march. "But there is still the signal fire to attend to, and the best place to set it going."

What would Miriam have done without the other woman's particular skills? She'd settled the guards' hash single-handed, and guided them to that headland. Miriam confirmed Thrax's whereabouts by walking back a short ways into the jungle, where she heard its cries and caught flashes of tawny motion against the dense green foliage.

"Lead the way, then," Miriam said, on returning, "down to the beach."

"What is out there, *Khun*, that you feel we need no guard at our back?"

"Thrax, that killed the Golden Dragon."

The woman peered earnestly into Miriam's face, and then she made that bow with her palms pressed together. "If Thrax is how you would be named, *Khun*. These women put no trust in me, not stand for us both going."

Miriam leaned against a still sun-warmed boulder considering, but the younger women were already pushing to their feet. She'd been sent there for Anna Lovell, and must keep the privileged woman's safety foremost in her mind.

"Can a fire be made here," Miriam asked, "among these rocks?"

"Sure a summit is best," the warrior woman said. "If you want be seen from afar. Draw attention from those close in too."

More than ever in life Miriam would have welcomed a wise head to give her counsel, someone with whom she could argue the feasibility and consequences of various plans. But she was alone and in self-imposed command of these women. One warrior, one Malay woman whose youth was stolen, nine young ladies unfortunate enough to be in the wrong place during an evil time, and one rich woman—at least by comparison with the rest.

"Make the fire here then, at the highest point you can possibly do." Miriam tried to sound as though she knew exactly what she was about, rather than trembling inside. "Should we all help gather fuel?"

Anna Lovell and the Bengali lady were the most timid and brought in the least amount of dry leaves and dead undergrowth, but even they wouldn't be left behind when the party plunged back into the jungle to forage. The warrior built a fire pit in a depression between boulders. By the time full darkness was upon them, the women had piled up a great store of tinder and faggots.

"Light it before the moon rises," Miriam told the woman. She was conscious of giving orders she couldn't carry out on her own, having no more idea of fire starting than of putting guards to the sword.

Soon the black woman kindled a respectable blaze, the fire crackled and hissed. Miriam watched Anna Lovell, Lan, and the others shrink away so they wouldn't be illuminated, like mice conveniently mouse-holing.

When the flames were reaching high into the dark tropical night, Miriam unwound the scarves from about her waist that she'd worn since leaving Hong Kong. Slowly and at intervals she cast them one by one into the fire. Impregnated with a decoction of strontium, orpiment, and saltpeter formulated by Saramago, the cloths combusted in tall showers of colored sparks. The women's eyes were fixed on the spectacle, and on her, Miriam realized. She leaned over the fire like a witch and, had they but known it, there was even her own familiar lurking in the forest.

By the time the moon rose and the stars shone numerous and brilliant in the heavens, Miriam had used up her pyrotechnic arsenal. She'd been sitting for some time clasping her knees to her chest, with the dying fire before her, and her back to a boulder.

"We'll let it burn as long as the fuel holds out," Miriam told the black warrior. They'd already given themselves away, but of course she'd never say so out loud.

In any case it was understood between them, and the other woman appointed herself sentry and took up a position atop one of the tallest boulders to watch over them. Most of the women were stretched out sleeping on the bare ground. She was eyeing a patch of dirt, ready to do the same, when Anna Lovell rose and came and sat next to her.

Miriam thought it was time Anna was told the news. "Your uncle, Baron Van der Capellen sent me."

"Dear old Uncle Cappy!" Anna cried, and broke down sobbing.

Miriam put her arm around Anna's shoulders and patted her, and then leaned back and studied the glory of stars overhead. She remembered the comfort in faith and the natural world.

Anna mastered herself, sniffling. "Did he tell you I was betrothed? On my way to be married."

Miriam nodded. "To the captain of *Dageraad*."

Anna went into fresh wails. The women nearest woke and turned anxious faces toward her.

"What will become of me?" Anna cried.

"Be calm, be silent, be strong," Miriam said. "The ship I signaled will come, with the blessing, and carry us all to Hong Kong."

"With the blessing! I am ruined, damaged, no decent man will want me now."

Ask her why she not drunk on opium like the rest.

Sexual favors in exchange for better treatment, such a thing was not unknown. Miriam thought hard about what to say next. "You must want you. Take the time you need to recover, then decide if you will honor this captain of *Dageraad*. There is no ruined or damaged in it, you did what you had to, to survive. And that is between you and your God."

"Oh!" Anna threw her arms round Miriam. "I knew you were a Christian woman the moment I laid eyes on you."

Miriam sighed, at the same time she circled both arms round Anna and returned her embrace. People would see what they wanted to see, and believe what pleased them best.

CHAPTER FIFTEEN

Dawn was near when Miriam woke, gazing up at the southern stars in a sky beginning to pale at the horizon. She rose, patted dirt from her clothes, and made her way carefully to the sentry keeping vigil on the summit. The woman was facing eastward toward the sea and the beach below the cliff they perched on, away from the jungle she'd watched through an anxious night.

She turned a weary face to Miriam. "What I wouldn't give for a proper wash, *Khun,* and to perform morning prayers."

Tears rose to Miriam's eyes, for the faith and resiliency of the woman. "I am no captain, my sister, my name is Miriam. There is the ocean, go down and wash. I will keep watch."

The black woman rose, stretching her muscled arms and legs, weapons thumping against her chest.

"Come with me, Maryam, and repeat the *shahadah.*"

So strong was Miriam's desire to be cleansed and make a profession of faith and gratitude, that she abandoned the advantage of their high perch and followed the black woman down the twisting path. The other woman had to assist Miriam in several difficult downward scrambles. Barely visible at first, the path to the beach became easier to follow as light crept into the world.

Reaching the beach at last, a mania of freedom overtook them. Miriam and the black woman raced to the water, throwing off their clothes like children as they ran. They plunged into the warm sea naked, except the black woman brought the sheathed *parang* in her teeth. Miriam dove and ran her hands through her hair, and rubbed them over her body, reveling in the clear water. She surfaced and turned toward shore, and beheld a sight that made her smile.

The women were coming down to the beach from the cliff top in a straggling line, the younger more nimble ones helping the laggards. Miriam recognized the short squat figure of Lan in the rear. Far behind and up the path, gliding along from boulder to boulder, was the Hell-Cat.

"What is it, makes your face glad?" the black woman asked, appearing at Miriam's side in the crystalline surf. "Merciful God! A jungle cat!"

Miriam put a restraining hand on the other woman's shoulder as she unsheathed the *parang* and took an overhand grip.

"That is Thrax, the reason I believed us guarded in the night. It was in the jungle."

The woman relaxed a fraction beside her, amazement on her face as she followed the progress of the women and their strange protector.

"I felt its eyes on me all night, but no menace. No threat did I feel." The woman turned a grave gaze on Miriam. "Why did you say *it, Khun?*"

"Because a Hell-Cat is neither male or female."

After a pause, the woman said, "That is how I want to be. Neither man nor woman."

"Just yourself." Miriam shook her head. What the other woman had endured Miriam wouldn't pretend to understand. "Tell me what I am to call you."

"Krunk," was the woman's simple answer.

Bright and hopeful rays of sunshine lit Miriam and Krunk from behind as they stood gently swaying with the motion of the warm surf.

"There are no snakes in the waters round the Dragon Islands this time of year," Miriam said. She watched Anna

Lovell, Lan, and the rest reach the beach and run to the waters edge. "Well, Krunk, off to dress and then to our prayers."

From his seat in the stern of the gig, Maximus Thorpe strained for a glimpse of Miriam on the strand. As the boat rose on the swell, Maximus and his gig's crew caught sight of a cluster of women in the water, holding hands. Among them Maximus didn't find Miriam. The ache at his heart he'd been experiencing of late became more intense.

When the group of women spotted two boats coming at them at top speed, they turned as one and rushed out of the surf. Maximus, acting as his own coxswain, followed the direction of the women's flight with his eye. Up the beach near a cliff and a fall of boulders, Miriam and a black person were praying.

Maximus watched them, his heart pounding, guiding the gig by instinct with his hand on the tiller. He'd been studying the Islamic faith and reading the Q'uran, at least those passages that Francis Blackwell translated.

"Lay on your oars," Maximus called when the gig was poised to run through the surf on to the beach.

Miriam and her companion were facing Mecca and the Ka'ba, and Maximus watched the woman he loved kneel and touch her forehead to the coral sand. He looked away; her prayers and her faith were private. Maximus wished he could command his men not to stare either.

A great deal of ogling and goggling was taking place in his gig as the men gazed after the fleeing ladies. In command of the cutter, Mr. Dashwood shot past the gig and ground ashore, scattering the women like skittles.

The women, all dark haired saving one, shrieked and ran away up the beach. Miriam rose to her feet, covered her face with her hands one last time, bowed toward Mecca, and walked forward to meet them.

Maximus gave a vigorous shout of, "Pull away!" barely containing the bubbling happiness rising within him.

The two groups met midway up the beach between the breaking surf and the cliff face. The party of men was led by Maximus and Mr. Dashwood, and that of the women by an odd trio consisting of Miriam, flanked by a fair-haired woman with an upturned nose, and a black person with a *kris* firmly in hand.

"Captain Thorpe, Mr. Dashwood," Miriam cried, "well met! Allow me to present Miss Anna Lovell."

Bows and curtseys were exchanged, somewhat ludicrous in the setting. Miriam presented the ladies gathered round in summary fashion. And it was discovered that Anna Lovell could speak English. When Admiral Baron Van der Capellen was mentioned, Anna burst into tears. Communications broke down and a confusion of languages ensued. Maximus heard Miriam trying to reassure the ladies in Malay, that the man with the red hair was no demon. They had not escaped the claws of the Golden Dragon to be flung into the teeth of a foreign devil. Meanwhile all Maximus wanted in life were a few minutes alone with Miriam.

"What is the name of Mai's daughter?" Miriam asked of a stout older woman. "The one who was exchanged for me?"

"That one? Her name Huong."

"Listen to me." Miriam raised her hands, palms outward, to the women crowded round. "You must go in these two boats to a larger ship, and then you shall be returned to your own people. Like Huong was to Mai."

Amazement and dawning hope spread over the faces of the young women belonging to the Boat People. No one spoke the Bengali lady's language, and she hugged herself and peered earnestly into their faces.

Miriam's tone became somewhat less confident. "I daresay the British consul in Hong Kong will do his best for those who do not have people near at hand."

"Vell, I don't care to vait round dis place longer." Anna Lovell took Mr. Dashwood's arm with a proprietary air.

Anna Lovell, of the buttercup yellow hair, led the way in settling on a seat in the cutter. The eight young ladies of the Boat People jumped in after her like cats, and turned expectant faces to Miriam.

"Miss Mir...that is to say, Miss Albuyeh." Maximus bowed to her with a blush. "May I be having a private word, if you please?"

When Miriam took the first steps to accompany him up the beach to the screen of a convenient boulder, the eight young women leaped out of the cutter and began to follow, screeching at Anna Lovell to remove from the boat as well.

"Vat?" Anna crossed her arms under her bosom. "Me, I am staying put."

Though he'd never spoken Malay on his quarterdeck, Maximus turned to the women and put the same tone of command he was accustomed to use there into his voice. "We will keep within your sight, ladies, I assure you. Seat yourselves in these two boats and we shall all depart directly."

Maximus left the pack of them behind, allowing Miriam to lead him up the beach. Most of the women began taking seats in the cutter, preferring handsome Mr. Dashwood to Saramago and the ill-favored crew of the gig.

In the anxious days of separation, Maximus half convinced himself he was not to see Miriam again. He was arranging his emotions beforehand, in the way of the Service, for the loss of brother officers and valued friends. Maximus's heart was aglow walking behind her and gazing on her straight back, the elegant way she moved, and on her luxurious long dark hair. His great good fortune and the circumstances under which he might next see her like this, with her hair down, occurred to him and moved Maximus deeply. Persian poetry rose to his mind.

> Was ever woman mistress of thy soul?
> When joy has thrilled through every glowing nerve,
> Hadst thou no wish that feeling to preserve?
> Does not a woman's love delight, entrance,
> And every blessing fortune yields enhance?

Such was Maximus's state of mind when Miriam halted and turned to him, and he feared his voice would come out a squeak. Then he took in her bruised face and cried, "Miriam m'dear! Who has been abusing you? Was it that black Amazon savage?"

A surprised expression passed over Miriam's face, and then—what he disliked of all things—an admonishing look came into her eyes. "Of course not, we could not pray together and stand side by side if that were the case. But do you think Krunk is Amazonian? Oh! Max...Captain Thorpe, I have so much to tell you."

"I wish you would, but first...May I?" he held out his arms and hoped, almost closing his eyes.

Miriam walked right into them, and lay her head on his chest. Maximus closed his arms gratefully round her.

"God is Merciful," she said. "You don't know how I prayed the exit strategy would succeed."

"We saw the signal from twenty-five leagues away. You must not make too much of how well Saramago's scarves worked. It will be going to his head."

She laughed a little and stepped away from him with a self-conscious glance toward the boats, where instantly many heads turned in another direction.

Maximus searched for the pretty speech he'd meant to make. But seeing him gazing stupidly at her, Miriam piped up. "It was the Golden Dragon did this to me, hit me, terrorized me, but in the end...You are not to look at me with such pity in your eyes, sir, I was not violated. I shall say that to you plain. Others," Miriam cut her eyes at the group of women in the boats, "suffered far worse treatment."

"The Golden Dragon is no ship, you will be telling me?"

"Not a ship, no. An evil power-mad little woman sitting on the next island over, poised at the center of her web like a spider."

"It pains me much you should have been subjected to such a creature," Maximus said. "I would very much like to hear the whole. For my own part, I have only one thing to say to ye." Maximus inhaled and drew himself up. "I want to share whatever part of your life you are willing to give me. If you would do me the honour of becoming my temporary wife, or permanent one, whichever and for how long shall always be at your own choosing."

Miriam smiled at him in such a tender affectionate way, the knot in Maximus's chest permanently unwound. She took his arm for the stroll back to the boats. Maximus would have liked another embrace, maybe a kiss to seal the bargain. But he realized a public display was beyond the ken of the demure woman by his side, who'd fought a Dragon and won.

She'd not battled alone, however, for when they arrived at the boats all smiles, Miriam immediately cried out, "But where is Krunk?"

The black Amazon was not seated in either of the two boats.

"Miss Lovell said, the Hottentot is to stay behind." Mr. Dashwood pointed helpfully up the beach, where Krunk was laboring toward the foot of the trail.

Miriam whirled on Maximus. "Oh no, not if I have anything to say to it!"

She marched out of the surf. Maximus caught up to her, of course he went after her.

"If you leave Krunk behind, you may as well leave Thrax and me." Miriam's pale cheek was flushed. "Thrax killed the Golden Dragon, and Krunk her guards, and that is the only reason I am with you today."

They reached the Amazonian together, out of breath.

"You will come with us, will you not Krunk?" Miriam said. "To the ship *Nonesuch*? This is her captain. Captain Thorpe is the only real *Khun* here. A most worthy one."

Miriam gave him such a look, Maximus Thorpe thought, as would wrench the heart of a stone.

"For that I will take your word, Maryam. All I shall ever need."

Krunk rose from sitting on a boulder as though she would bow, wobbled and staggered. Maximus caught Krunk up in his arms, weapons and all, and carried the warrior to the boats. He deposited the Amazonian in the bow of the gig. The gig's crew stared at him open mouthed, then as one gave a cry of surprise. Down the beach raced a tawny colored creature the size of an overfed house cat.

Maximus gave his hand to Miriam, and she was settling beside him in the stern, when Thrax came pelting through the surf, swimming at the last. Maximus reached out over the gunwale and grabbed the cat by the scruff.

"This would be yours then, Madam," Maximus said with dignity, as he deposited the wet animal in Miriam's lap. "And a fine job it has done, protecting its mistress."

"Thank you, Maximus," Miriam said for his ear alone, with a meaning glance forward at her black companion and one hand on the Hell-Cat.

CHAPTER SIXTEEN

In six weeks of cruising following the rescue of the women from the Dragon islands, HMHV *Nonesuch* successfully reunited six of the young women of the Boat People with their friends. Miriam made it known that this she would see done before returning to Hong Kong. Her determination, which instantly had the backing of *Nonesuch's* captain, ran contrary to Anna Lovell's desire to reach that settlement without delay. The Boat People might fetch their daughters from Kowloon or Hong Kong, Anna loudly proclaimed, while Miriam and Maximus knew they could never do so without exposing themselves to being taken up for piracy.

A solution came along that stopped the survivors of the Golden Dragon from throttling one another. The steam ship HMHV *Spartan* was sent to rendezvous with *Nonesuch*.

In *Spartan's* great cabin, wearing a *hijab* and playing the part of just another woman caught in the Golden Dragon's slave trade, Miriam gave her account to the ship's captain and marine officers of the criminality centered in the Dragon islands. She tried to impress on them the fact that some of the men to be found on Dragon Island were prisoners and not pirates—local fishermen and Boat People who'd fallen foul of the Golden Dragon. Even with Maximus standing stolidly by her chair to loan countenance to her tale, Miriam had a strong impression the eager sea-officers only attended to one thing. They must not burn down the local huts, until all the plundered merchandize was got out of them.

Captain Newcombe of *Spartan* said, "Very good, madam, I thank you." And with that dismissed Miriam, and turned to Maximus. "May I have the pleasure of your company for supper aboard this evening, Captain Thorpe? Do bring Baron Van der Capellen's niece. I understand you have the lady with you. After what she's been through I expressly wish to extend her every comfort and accommodation *Spartan* has to offer."

Miriam thought the top of Maximus's head was going to blow off, and she jumped to her feet. All foreign and uncomprehending, she wrung Captain Newcombe's hand. Maximus managed a stiff bow and salute, and stomped out of *Spartan's* great cabin. He sat there steaming in his gig on the pull back to *Nonesuch*, the color of his skin matching his fiery hair. The gig's crew, even Saramago, kept their eyes on their oars and the sea lane between the vessels.

Maximus sent Miriam up the side of *Nonesuch* before him, never touching her, allowing the hands at the gangway to assist her. He returned the salutes of the officers and then, turning to Miriam, burst out, *"Air mheùd 's a their na slòigh, cha ghlòir a dhearbhas ach gnìomh."*[1]

She could only guess he'd uttered a string of invective in Gaelic. Mr. Dashwood, the officer of the watch, shook his head. The first lieutenant shrugged, with a knowing purse of his lips as though he'd suspected Captain Thorpe of irregularity all along.

Miriam made the quarterdeck a bob and taking Maximus's arm, she pulled him to the after hatchway companion ladder. She preceded him down the ladder to his little den in the gunroom. Once there, she closed the canvas door and led him to a seat beside her on a chest.

"I don't mind it, Maximus, really I don't. I would rather eat rice on the floor of the great cabin here in *Nonesuch*

---

[1] For all the world will say, not words but deeds are proof.

with the Boat ladies left to us, than at that pompous ass's table."

Maximus snorted, and after a few deep breaths he was able to speak English again. "It is the ingratitude, the presumption, the infernal ignorance I cannot abide. How can you stomach it, and pretend it does not hurt you?"

His sympathy brought a lump of emotion into Miriam's throat, unexpected and hard to swallow down. "I've had some experience in being taken for a lesser being. I always try to turn presumption and infernal ignorance to my advantage."

He turned to her and she came under scrutiny of those intense and weird eyes. "You are the wonder of the world, Miriam m'dear. If it were me I should have grabbed Newcombe by his starched frill and yelled into his face, it was I as saved that great baby, Van der Capellen's niece."

Oh! if only, Miriam thought. "Maybe some day, one fine day. But for the now, this is how Lord Q wants it—"

"Aye! Lord Q, damn his eyes! Must we be slaves to the will of a man thousands of leagues away in London?"

As yet that spider sitting at the center of his own web those thousands of miles away had only asked her to do what Miriam viewed as worthy and necessary work. In the process introducing her to a worthy man, and his incomparable ship.

"Yes," Miriam said. "When his will coincides with my own."

Maximus shook his head, but a gentler light came into his eyes. "And I suppose you and Lord Q would be meaning me to escort Miss Anna Lovell to supper without you? She of the golden hair, and important connections."

"That is the way of the world, or at least your half of it." Miriam squeezed his hand. "Anna will make you a charming table companion. And you are to consider while you are doing the civil, Captain Newcombe said he means to offer her every accommodation aboard his ship. If we can once be rid of her, we can cruise at our leisure and you may return to your private quarters."

He gave her a sidelong glance and returned the pressure of her hand. "I believe I can reconcile myself to the duty, especially if you will be allowing a wee kiss."

"If my will coincides with your own?"

"The only way it can be between us."

Tingling with anticipation Miriam put her arms round Maximus's broad shoulders, prepared to return his kisses and caresses one for one. Since that was how it was to be between them.

In the great cabin of *Nonesuch* Anna Lovell was cheek by jowl with women she considered her inferiors and, what was worse, who knew an uncomfortable fact or two about her. She didn't hesitate to accept Captain Newcombe's offer to carry her aboard *Spartan,* and never returned to *Nonesuch* after the supper party. Anna sent across for her few belongings and the Bengali lady to act as chaperone and companion, Miriam insisted, not as her maid. *Spartan,* carrying the Dutch Admiral Baron Van der Capellen's favorite sister's daughter, steamed off to do her work of salvage and destruction in the Dragon islands. It would be this portion of the fight against the South China Seas pirates that would later be recounted, in Dutch and English circles. Modern warfare and innovations triumphing over ancient savage ways.

A fortnight's sailing, with an excursion into the Bay of Tonkin, restored the two remaining Boat ladies to the bosoms of their families. The homes they returned to were floating households. *Nonesuch* was fortunate to find them plying in the vicinity of Hainan Island, a place of surpassing romantic beauty. What was not so romantic was the life the Boat People led, as Miriam beheld it while each lady said her good-byes and transferred to her family's vessel. Real joy shone on the faces of the mothers and numerous little siblings or cousins as the women went aboard, but Miriam thought she caught disappointment and an air of grievance among the men.

Her heart was heavy as Maximus set *Nonesuch's* course for Hong Kong. Miriam knew it shouldn't be, they'd all survived and gone home. Except Lan and Krunk, who were accompanying them to Hong Kong. Like Miriam they were homeless wanderers, a disheartening but unavoidable fact. In Iran there might be a place for her, but it was more likely the menfolk would be as dismayed at her return as the Boat People.

Miriam was making it her study to control her insecurity over whether she had a home aboard *Nonesuch*. Maximus, bless him, was positive on that score. He was *Nonesuch's* captain, his word was law at sea—or so she'd heard. But they were not always to be at sea, and that was the source of her trouble as the ship sailed for Hong Kong. In Hong Kong they would meet Francis, and other representatives of the British Crown. Miriam's heart beat faster at the thought, the notion of a new mission, of another assignment from Lord Q.

The captain of *Nonesuch*, that wonderous ship and flight in her, quickened Miriam's pulse too. His flame-colored hair and mismatched eyes—the result, Miriam believed, of injury—made him unique. That was merely the outside of the man, of more importance to Miriam was his willingness to take her as she was. Or to try. She with her "this is what I don't want," speeches, a woman of no family and no country. At present what sank Miriam's spirits most was the possibility Lord Q, and the diplomatic and military establishments, would not like her becoming *sigheh* to Captain Maximus Thorpe. It was far more than likely, she was still considered not one of them. *Nonesuch* could be taken from him, or worse he might be made to choose.

"What furrows your brow so, Miriam m'dear?" Maximus asked.

"I think someday, I will think myself to death."

"'Daughters of Persia!'" Maximus quoted with a slight smile. "'Still is yours the art to charm, while life endures.'"

Miriam was surprised and pleased. "You've been reading in Persian poetry, I find."

"All that your step-father would give me in translation. I should like to read the Q'uran in the original Arabic, if you had the patience to teach me."

He didn't realize what he asked, the obligation he placed her under, nor how much his assumption they should be together so long touched her. Miriam went and took his hand, for they were alone in the great cabin. What would she give, what would she not do to keep this life? Miriam wondered if Maximus knew the ending of that poem. "Thus whether beautiful or plain, woman asserts her lordly reign, which proves her intellectual power—for wisdom is the sex's dower!"

The straits between Kowloon on the mainland of China and the island of Hong Kong were crowded with an astonishing number of sampans and fishing boats, even that most ancient variety using cormorants tied to a complex system of lines like the netting round *Nonesuch's* balloons. After maneuvering through these obstacles, *Nonesuch* made her way into the harbor outside the settlement of Hong Kong. *Queen Charlotte*, Lord Exmouth's flag ship, was there swaying to her cables large as life. The flag put a boat in the water once *Nonesuch* was at single anchor. Miriam and Maximus exchanged glances and went together to the great cabin to shift into visiting clothes.

Queen Charlotte's flag lieutenant came aboard, saluted *Nonesuch's* quarterdeck, and shook hands with Maximus. They stood together in conference a few moments, then Maximus's head came up in surprise and he turned round to his crew.

"Mr. Dodd, pass the word for the Dragon Island survivors, they are requested and required aboard the flag."

Krunk stepped forward from the fringes of the afterguard at the summons. Miriam had discovered Krunk's wish to remain with her as a sort of aide-de-camp, and to live for the present as a man. "Since I cannot be *it*, like your beast. I be more use working on this ship. And fighting." Only Miriam had a grasp of what gender Krunk was, from a natural philosophy perspective. Seaman Bora's vacant place in the afterguard was thus filled. A blackguardly set of men even for that ship the afterguard was overawed by Krunk's fierce appearance, and kept at a respectful distance.

Saramago was sent by Mr. Dodd to ferret Lan out of the galley. Maximus excused himself to the flag lieutenant and stepped over to Miriam. Once the old ayah was on deck, looking round in confusion at the newcomers to the ship, Krunk and *Queen Charlotte's* flag lieutenant both bore down on Maximus and Miriam.

"What is this, Maryam?" Krunk asked. "Where the boat take us? You come with us, or not?"

Maximus and the flag lieutenant began speaking at the same time.

"Mr. Flowers, allow me to present—" Maximus began.

"Miss Kodio Blackwell, I presume?" the flag lieutenant said.

Miriam curtsied, and the flag lieutenant withdrew a large limp letter from his jacket pocket and handed it to her. From another pocket Mr. Flowers took an official packet in tarred canvas cover and presented it to Maximus.

"You are not required aboard *Queen Charlotte* at this time, Miss Blackwell," Mr. Flowers said in a low voice, giving Krunk a suspicious glance. "The Admiral wishes to interview the *native* survivors. I am sure you have not yet remarked it, sir," the lieutenant said in a louder tone to Maximus, "*Spartan* preceded your arrival by two days. We know all about the encounter with that vicious band of pirates. It is long since past time they were put down."

"What he saying?" Krunk said.

"You have a thing or two to learn about the Navy, Krunk," Maximus said in stern Malay. "You will go with this officer, along with the old *frau* over there, and speak when you are spoken to. They will have an interpreter over there, you may be sure."

"And then?" Krunk demanded. "We stay, the slaves of *farang* instead of Golden Dragon?"

"Mr. Flowers," Maximus said in English. Miriam moved discreetly next to Krunk to translate. "This seaman, who has signed on aboard *Nonesuch*, is concerned about being returned to her. And as I am short of hands, I should like your assurance you will be bringing both of the former captives back to *Nonesuch*."

"Aye, aye, Captain Thorpe. Of course." Mr. Flowers simpered and bowed. "What would his lordship want with those two ill-looking brutes once he's had his questions answered."

Miriam didn't feel obliged to translate this last part for Krunk. "I know Lord Exmouth," she said. "You will be safe, you will be returned to this ship. He is an honorable man, a gentleman."

"The lion is known by scratch of his claw." Krunk eyed Mr. Flowers' pale sweating face with distaste, but followed him into *Queen Charlotte's* boat.

Miriam's attention was divided between her companions in the boat and the letter in her hand, which bore Francis's script. She stole furtive glances at Maximus, who was turning the official packet over and over in his hands as though trying to judge its content by feel.

After they'd watched the distant figures crawl up the side of *Queen Charlotte*, Maximus offered her his arm. "Should you like to go below and take a glass of wine, while we open our letters?"

Seated in a chair in the great cabin, with Thrax on her lap and Maximus standing before her, Miriam said, "What I should like of all things is Saramago's fortifying tea."

Maximus instantly called out for his steward, and then Miriam broke the seal of her letter and Maximus untied the string round the canvas packet.

"These are orders." Maximus withdraw an oiled silk envelope from the packet. "If you will permit me."

He half bowed to Miriam and ducked into his private sleeping cabin, closing the door behind him.

Miriam unfolded her letter, written on unmarked parchment, not Consul Francis Blackwell's official stationary.

"Hong Kong Harbour
Aboard Queen Charlotte

Dearest Daughter Merry,

You cannot imagine the Joy it gave me to learn from Spartan's coming in that you were well and aboard HMHV Nonesuch. Very soon I hope to do myself the honour of expressing to you the depth of my happiness at your return, and my suffering in your absence—along with other of your Friends. For the moment I confine myself to a brief remark and an invitation.

Aboard Queen Charlotte there has been a most unusual tale recounted to the Admiral by a certain Young Person. I wonder you should have let her out of your sight, her rescue being your *raison d'être* in these parts, choosing instead to attend to persons who can have no direct bearing on your cause." Miriam paused, growing angry, wondering what Francis conceived of as 'her cause'. She read on. "Had you attended her to Hong Kong, I am sure there could have been no wild tales. As it was, I was obliged, before his lordship's good opinion was entirely lost, to remind the Young Person that she may be a Dutch admiral's niece, but you are a British ambassador's daughter. Though that put a period to matters for the moment, you will better comprehend his lordship's summons for questioning of the other survivors carried aboard Nonesuch.

I thought it wise to request to be present at his lordship's interviews though I trust the natives will have nothing to Add, and we have come through the worst unpleasantness. I will move on to what gives me greater satisfaction. Please come to me at the Embassy. Your Family—attended by another Party—is here, Merry, and eager to receive you once more into its Embrace. I hope you believe I remain,

Your Devoted Father,
Francis"

Miriam read the letter through several times. She was obliged to stop her furious stroking of Thrax, lest she raise a spark from its fur. Saramago walked in with the welcome glasses of coca tea.

Maximus emerged from his cabin, and without a word Miriam handed him Francis's note.

"It is a most singular letter," Maximus said, folding and extending the letter back to Miriam.

She'd given it him to read with that intimacy and unrestraint that was growing between them. The last part of Francis's letter rang in her memory, and Miriam found it hard to concentrate on anything else.

"Lord Exmouth surely is not here in Hong Kong on Anna Lovell's account?"

"Nay, I doubt it. Something is afoot. The Chinese perhaps, disliking our recent activities in these waters. Sir Edward must be here attending to that, and he has sent on my orders." Maximus took a seat on a locker near her armchair. "*Nonesuch* is to rendezvous with another vessel at such a time and place, that I must leave in a day or two to keep it. If not to-day itself, as I cannot be counting on finding weather."

It would have been apparent to a meaner intellect than Miriam's that the particulars of his orders were being purposely withheld. She became aware Thrax was tensed in her lap, a cruel hard sheen in its yellow eyes as it stared at Maximus. Miriam was reminded she must be careful in her intimate relationships, lest the consequences become irreversible.

"I understand perfectly." Miriam didn't at all comprehend whether she or *Nonesuch* held greater sway over his heart. "You will go with me this evening to meet Francis and my...Do you know, I have an unreasoning dread my mother has come for me."

"Of course I shall attend you, if you wish it. You've no idea how much I am in sympathy with your fear of a roaring irrational parent."

Maximus put his hand up in an unconscious gesture and cupped it over his pale colored, damaged eye.

CHAPTER SEVENTEEN

Bolstered by a great deal of Saramago's coca *maté* Miriam entered the Embassy lobby with its gently turning fans. She and Maximus gave their names and were immediately admitted by a marine sentry to the Consul's chamber. Miriam took a fortifying breath and walked in, but finding there only three gentlemen she exhaled in relief. No woman who would slap her with her small hands. Demons, she'd learned, come in many guises.

"Miriam! Oh, dearest Miriam. All is forgiven, you may come home now!"

Haris Reza was, as ever, full of conceit and a pushing self sufficiency.

"How do you do, Haris?" Miriam said.

She tried to move past Haris Reza to give her hand to Francis, and embrace her brother Farrokh. Those two were standing shoulder to shoulder, shifting uneasily. Francis was scowling as though there were a disagreeable odor in the air, and Farrokh avoided her eye.

"Miriam dear! Didn't you hear me? You are forgiven for running away, you will not be punished if you will but come home with me. *I* still wish to be your—"

At this point in his importuning Haris tried to grasp Miriam's hand, and found himself hip checked by a large Scotsman. An ugly one too, or so the distaste on Haris Reza's face suggested. Miriam stumbled past them and fell into an embrace with Farrokh, extending one hand to Francis Blackwell.

"*Salaam alay-kum*," Farrokh said.

"*Walay-kum salaam*, Farrokh," Miriam said.

Up until the traditional greeting they'd been speaking Farsi. Maximus was standing by with a quizzical expression, though clearly disliking Haris Reza's wilder freaks.

"Farrokh, allow me to present Captain Maximus Thorpe of His Majesty's ship *Nonesuch*. Captain Thorpe, my brother, Farrokh Albuyeh Kodio."

The two men shook hands, Farrokh adding, "Of Shah Khaqan's Royal Guard." Maximus went next to give his hand to Francis Blackwell. Haris Reza, meanwhile, was trying to insinuate himself in the spaces between them.

"Captain Thorpe," Miriam said, suppressing a sigh, "this is Haris Reza, my mother's friend. Haris, Captain Maximus Thorpe. Let us speak English now, if you please. Farrokh, how surprised I am to find you here."

"I came half way round the world only to see you were safe, my sister," Farrokh said, holding Miriam's hand.

Miriam kissed her younger brother, and Haris Reza exploded.

"No kisses for me, Miriam, dearest? Your own betrothed?"

Maximus's eyes widened, and then narrowed to different colored slits.

"The only place we are betrothed, Haris," Miriam said, "is in my mother's mind."

"'Can scorn that beauteous brow defile?'" Haris cried.

"Can you imagine crossing the Atlantic and Indian Oceans with that?" Farrokh said, to no one in particular.

"'I would not for the world that thou, shouldst feel the torture I do now,'" Haris continued quoting Persian poetry in a loud tone, "'From morn till eve, and eve till morn, I wander desolate, forlorn—'"

Another grab for Miriam's upper arm this time, and Maximus again interposed. "You are making the lady uncomfortable, Mr. Reza. I suggest you take a step back."

"How dare you! Take your hands off me," Haris cried, to all their surprise, for Maximus hadn't touched him. "I am the lady's mother's trusted friend. Who are you? Miriam, who is this ill-mannered, ill-looking foreign brute?"

Something snapped inside Miriam. She bore down on Haris Reza, grasped him by his shirt front, and dealt him a double slap. One direction, back again! Nothing ever felt so satisfying; the expression of Haris Reza's face, the small whoops she thought she heard from the other men.

"This man, I cannot say his name in the same breath as yours, Haris," Miriam said. "Captain Thorpe is my husband,"—gasps from the men, even, Miriam was aware, from Maximus—"so my advice to you is, go back to Iran."

"Oh Miriam! Will you throw away your beauty, your substance, your life on this—" Haris thought better of what he was about to say, when Miriam took a menacing step toward him. He fell back on poetry. "'I will wander desolate, forlorn; no eye to pity, voice to bless, none to relieve my wretchedness.'"

"You've come a long way trying to give my mother what she wanted," Miriam said, "and for that I'm sorry. But I would not wander, no, I would hasten back to Iran. What my mother wants changes daily. Just ask Mr. Blackwell."

Miriam wished she could take back that last remark, not wanting to cause Francis pain. Francis Blackwell, however, bowed in wholehearted agreement, as though vindicated.

"Come, Haris," Farrokh said. "There is nothing to be done. In the morning I will help you find a ship for the voyage home."

"Do you give up so easily?" Haris put his hands on his slender hips. "I do not. I do not believe in this marriage. What dower did you receive, what dower could you have possibly received?"

"You are become impertinent, Sir," Maximus said in a thundering voice.

Farrokh chose to take pity on Haris Reza, who, everyone could see, would be easily slaughtered by the Captain. "Peace, my friends, no need for violence. Miriam is safe, secure, and wed. As her closest male relative, I am satisfied. I wish you both happy."

Maximus and Farrokh shook hands again, fast friends, fellow men of war. Miriam refrained from rolling her eyes heavenward.

Haris cried, "Farrokh, Miriam! Do you care nothing for a mother's wishes? This is not what Zahraa wanted."

"One more word, Haris," Farrokh said, "and Mr. Blackwell, Captain Thorpe, and I shall take turns holding you while m'sister punches."

At this delicate juncture a tap sounded at the door, and the marine sentry stepped in bearing a letter for the captain of *Nonesuch* on a tray. Maximus took himself apart to read his letter. Farrokh and Francis, exchanging a nod, laid hold of Haris Reza, one on either side.

"Bid Miriam farewell, now, Haris," Farrokh said. "You shall tell our mother you last saw her well and happy, but *you* shall not be seeing more of her. That would not be proper in a married lady."

"Her duty now is to cleave to her husband," Francis added, unnecessarily.

When Maximus finished perusing his letter and stepped over to Miriam, Farrokh and Francis had not returned from bundling Haris into a palanquin back to their lodgings. She still needed to speak to Francis about Goh Cheng Cheng's grateful offer, to settle Nguyen Lan in a little establishment of her own.

"It is a summons from Sir Edward Pellew," Maximus said. "To come and give my report aboard *Queen Charlotte*."

"Am I to come too?" Miriam asked, feeling a little foolish, because she didn't want to be left with her family like any ordinary wife.

"The letter doesn't mention you, but you shall certainly come with me. My wife must be received wherever I am."

"About that, Maximus, er, Captain Thorpe," Miriam said, as Farrohk and Francis came back in. "Our connection must be kept private. That I am *sigheh* to you is a family matter, between you and I." Miriam glanced over at Francis, and at Farrohk's expectant face, and added with as much grace as she could summon, "And my people."

Maximus walked out of the Embassy unconvinced that not acknowledging his connection with Miriam was the best course. To him it smacked of dishonour. Maximus should be quite happy to let one and all know he was favored by an incomparable woman. And he wondered at the British Consul, her step-father or uncle or whatever, at his complaisance and agreement. Francis Blackwell no doubt was a deep old file, used to the diplomatic game. He'd given Maximus a strong hint that Miriam was a deeper one still. As to Miriam's brother Farrokh, he was no wiser than most soldiers of Maximus's acquaintance. It was clear to him which of the siblings came in for the lion's share of dash and wit.

For both Miriam's male relations it was that term *sigheh* that seemed to settle matters for them. Maximus suspected that was because the arrangement made it convenient for Miriam to leave him, if she chose, sometime in future.

Miriam took his arm for the walk to the quay, refusing a palanquin so they could speak along the way. Consequently they both arrived sweating through their clothing, though Maximus was more comfortable in spirit. *Nonesuch* was dear

Miriam's reason for secrecy. When Maximus confirmed to her the vessel was not his own but the property of government, he immediately followed her reasoning. That she should be put to such an expedient, Maximus felt, did him and his government little credit. Clearly Miriam's was the wise old head between them, she at least understood a man is not ruined while he has his ship.

"Sure you have persuaded me to your way of thinking, though I don't like it above half," Maximus said. He stopped short on the quay, before reaching *Nonesuch's* gig. "But I will no be allowing anyone to ignore and disrespect you, and so you will be accompanying me to call upon Sir Edward."

Sir Edward Pellew was clearly expecting Maximus alone, for when Miriam and Maximus were shown in to the flag captain's cabin where he was seated, they found him at his leisure with his breeches unbuttoned at the knee. Nevertheless, Sir Edward heaved his heavy frame up and came forward with surprise, a hint of pleasure, and curiosity on his face.

"Miss Miriam, how do you do?" Sir Edward cried, after exchanging salutes with Maximus. "This is an unexpected pleasure. McNutty!" Sir Edward glared down his nose at the flag captain's steward, who'd admitted a lady to his presence without any warning whatever. "A bottle of madeira with the yellow seal and rout-cakes, if you please."

After giving this order Sir Edward appeared easier. He became solicitous of Miriam, leading her to a chair, and generally behaving as if both Miriam and Maximus were expected and invited. Then his lordship nearly wrecked on a lee shore.

"My dear Miss Miriam, how glad I am to see you. And in such very fine looks too. One would hardly credit that you've been—that is to say—you survived..." Sir Edward left off in confusion, clearly on the verge of congratulating Miriam on having not been too much raped and abused. He'd not risen to flag rank without the ability to change tacks, however, and Sir Edward said, "I hope I see you well, quite well. Francis Blackwell told me your brother is lately arrived. He will oblige you to go home, no doubt."

"I am just come from visiting my brother Farrokh, and Francis, thank you for asking, Sir Edward. Captain Thorpe was good enough to see me to the Embassy for the reunion, which is where your letter found him. I must beg your pardon for intruding on your notice, I should never have come aboard your ship uninvited except that Captain Thorpe chose to obey his duty at once."

Sir Edward blinked a couple of times. "You are very good, ma'am. Since you are so sensible of our duty, I will take Captain Thorpe away for the space of half a glass. For the ah...debriefing I called him to me for. Pray send for the steward should you require anything at all."

Maximus followed Sir Edward's wide backside up the ladder to the next deck, the Admiral's quarters were on a separate and higher level than the flag captain's cabin. He was not altogether easy about leaving Miriam sitting alone with cakes and a glass of wine she probably would not drink. Below decks seemed unusually deserted of activity, in Maximus's view, as though the officers and men had been made to keep away.

In the Admiral's great cabin, a noble apartment redolent of beeswax, Sir Edward went rather fussily round, adjusting lamps and opening doors and peering into his sleeping space and pantry, before inviting Maximus to a chair.

After Sir Edward cordially served him another glass of madeira, he desired Maximus's report on the exit strategy. This Maximus gave, and in conclusion he said, "*Nonesuch* is ideally suited to such work, Sir. The signal was clear as a bell from 25 leagues away at elevation."

"There is talk of using crack ships, among those who know such a thing exists," Sir Edward said, "of using them for overland recognizance. Think of the advantage of knowing your enemy's formation before battle. What do you say to it?"

"If you could get the right lift to carry you inshore, I should say it would be damned awkward landing in some farmer's field rather than the forgiving sea."

"You are very poetical," Sir Edward said. "Speaking of the right conditions, how do you find young Dashwood take to his duty?"

"A finer hand with the Mechanism I've never seen, and apart from that Mr. Dashwood himself is like a rare old weathercock. Now if I may be so bold, Sir Edward, I'd like to pose a question of me own."

Sir Edward nodded with an indulgent smile.

"What game is Lord Q playing at? Why the secrecy in my orders, and why is Miss Albuyeh ignored and not acknowledged for the service she has performed at great risk to her person? At Lord Q's particular bidding, I might add. Code Black is what I will be remembering."

The genial expression left Sir Edward's face. "Who would have supposed the Golden Dragon, that viper of rapacity, would have been a woman, eh? A small Oriental at that. Do you know how it—she—died?"

"Miri...ah, Miss Albuyeh said it was the Hell-Cat, knocked her down and ripped the throat right out of her."

"And you believe that tale, Maximus, an animal the size of a hedge pig?"

Maximus frowned. "And what tale would you be believing, Sir?"

"The one told by all three of the other survivors, and recollect that three people could not be more unalike. All agreed that it was Miriam who killed the Golden Dragon. Your seaman Krunk, who may be too bizarre even for your crew, saw the body. Throat torn out, but never a mention of a fabled cat. You just stated her clothes were covered in gore when you took her off the island, and her person bruised and battered."

"You cannot really think..." Maximus fell silent, remembering the pressure of Miriam's hand on his arm and the justice of her words on their walk to the quay. It would not do to defend her too vehemently. Maximus took a deep breath. "And so she is not to know the content of my orders because why—you suspect she is a savage murderess—yet Lord Q still wants to involve her in another mission?"

Sir Edward waived a hand. "I could say something pert like in Lord Q's business a savage murderess may be of more use than not, but I won't. We are not pert in the Navy, as you know very well. The secrecy is because there are too many unknowns and that is a thing his lordship cannot like. Will the young person agree to another mission or be taken away by her relatives? Will you carry her again knowing what she is? She seems to trust you, however, attending her to family meetings."

"I shall certainly undertake the mission, *Nonesuch* and I are ever at the disposal of Government." Maximus worked to keep the joy he felt from reaching his face. "Whether Miss Albuyeh will consent to another Code Black, is a matter for her to decide. If I were she, I would no risk it for an ungrateful nation." He gave Sir Edward a level stare. "Returning to *Nonesuch* and her crew, Sir, I will say that Mr. Dashwood is a capable first officer. But he has a deal to learn about the ship's ways and the people who work her. Someone just as promising for a crack ship's officer, is the young lady herself, Miss Miriam Albuyeh Kodio Blackwell." Thorpe, Maximus added with inward satisfaction.

Sir Edward choked, and almost spat out his wine. "Her? A woman, Maximus! Are you besotted, has your head been too long in the ether?"

Edward Pellew considered that only mutual esteem and long association kept Maximus Thorpe from coming to blows with him over his remarks. He'd put an official letter into Miriam's hand, and then seen them both over *Queen Charlotte's* side, attentive to any familiarity between them. Any little becks or glances or over solicitudes. None were shown, except when the gig had pulled a ways toward *Nonesuch*, Sir Edward did remark the two heads inclined together. Were he a score years younger he should like to be tête-à-tête with such a woman; beautiful, no fool, no quite the opposite, a luminous skin, eyes, and figure; but that was neither here nor there. The question that Lord Quondam put to him was whether Maximus was in fact besotted.

"I really could not say," Sir Edward said, uncomfortable before Lord Quondam, an unfeeling reptile incapable of appreciation of a beautiful woman or much of anything else resembling human feeling. "What do you collect? You heard all he said from the sleeping cabin."

Lord Quondam, an older man whose once ginger locks were now a pure white, stared at Sir Edward out of matching intense green eyes. "Not quite all, I stole down to have a look at our Miss. Having seen, and knowing what the lass is capable of, what I collect is if Maximus hasn't managed to capture her attention, he is no connection of mine."

"I thought you did not desire the connection?" Sir Edward's voice was strident. He was certain he'd been asked to warn Maximus as to the inappropriate foreignness of the young lady. "Maximus and Miss Miriam's connection I mean to say."

A ghost of a smile played over Lord Quondam's face, and he regarded Sir Edward as though he were a not very bright schoolboy. "You did not mistake me, I will not be approving of any love relationships. What would happen were I to let all my best operatives live happily ever after?"

Sir Edward could not like any of this. He reflected that he would far rather fight Barbary or South China Sea pirates or any number of fleet actions, than deal with his own country's foreign service and its peculiar machinations. "Then what's to be done?" he asked.

"Break them up, of course. This mission you've sent them on is admirably calculated to do just that."

"I've sent them on!" Sir Edward cried. "Pray do not honour me with any credit in your schemes, Lord Q."

A legitimate smile lit Lord Quondam's face, it seemed he did not dislike his sobriquet. Sir Edward couldn't understand Lord Quondam's treatment of Miriam, and more especially Maximus. Kind, generous, honest soul that he was, Sir Edward wished God might speed the young people away from a life of intrigue, spying, deception, and bedevilment.

CHAPTER EIGHTEEN

Mr. Dashwood found them weather, and Miriam was allowed to stand on the companion ladder, speaking trumpet in hand, to relay orders during the ascent. She was in full high altitude dress, including a new cap of alpaca wool and leather ear pieces Saramago had whipped up for her. Maximus was wrestling the yoke back when the larboard steering cable parted, throwing several of the seamen stationed there backwards in its wild trajectory. *Nonesuch* canted sharply to starboard. Miriam hung on with one hand to the companion ladder handrail, while in the other she clutched the speaking trumpet. She dangled for several seconds, until Mr. Dodd came pelting downstairs, knocking her loose of her hold and into the starboard bulkhead.

Among the larbowlines flung down, Krunk was getting to his feet. He pulled Miriam upright and gave her a shove back in the direction of the ladder. "She is like no ship I ever—"

Krunk didn't finish speaking because Maximus roared for the seamen to take stations for replacement of the steering cable. On deck Mr. Dashwood managed the scraps of canvas forward that kept *Nonesuch's* head before the oncoming gale. Miriam clung to the companion ladder rail with both hands, speaking trumpet clamped under one arm, trying to focus on the steering cable operation led by Maximus and Mr. Dodd. Partly to concentrate her mind after the great thumping she'd taken, Miriam felt a knot rising on her scalp already, and so that she might see Mr. Dodd coming next time.

In less than half a glass, as Miriam was learning to calculate time, the spare steering cable was in, another laid neatly along the deck for redundancy, and the ascent sequence started again. The ship's bows came up and up, Maximus wrestling the yoke, Mr. Dashwood clinging to the Mechanism when he wasn't running from lower deck to upper, while Miriam shouted the Captain's orders to adjust the stunsails. Then came the well remembered soaring up and settling down that caused Miriam's stomach to flutter.

The helm changed. Mr. Dodd ran down to take it, and Maximus went on deck to supervise the getting up of the flotation. Miriam tried to squeeze small on the ladder each time they passed.

"How do you do?" Maximus said, his voice full of concern, as he moved round her.

"Very well, Sir," she said, "I thank you."

Miriam had learned a thing or two about the Navy, and knew that was the only reply she could make unless she wanted Maximus to lose credit before his crew.

By the time the great balloons were filling, the air penetratingly cold, and the turbulent sea and winds left behind, Miriam did feel nearly well. Saramago brought her a second coca *maté* while the work of firing braziers and inflation began on deck. She sipped it through a silver pipette from a covered mug. The buffeting of air sounded against the ship's hull, and it grew quiet and colder still. Mr. Dashwood came half way down the ladder.

"We are at altitude, Mr. Dodd. Keep her very well thus." Mr. Dashwood turned to Miriam with a smile, and in a softer tone he said, "Miss Miriam, the Captain desires you will join him on deck with the atmospheric instruments."

Miriam staggered aft into the open space that was the great cabin, and took the instruments in their strapped cases from the racks on the bulkhead. She hung them by the straps crosswise over her body. The journal of atmospheric notations she put in a pocket of the canvas harness she wore over trowsers, gown, and greatcoat. God be Merciful, she thought, hauling her load up the companion ladder, and don't let me fall forward on my face this time.

Mr. Dashwood fastened her harness to the lifeline as soon as Miriam's foot touched the upper deck.

"Captain Thorpe is right forward, ma'am," Mr. Dashwood said with some gravity. And then he burst out, "This is my first love! Is it not the glory of the world? Hahaha!"

"It is, Mr. Dashwood. It is, indeed." Miriam's knuckles were turning white gripping the lifeline.

She clamped shut her chattering teeth and shuffled forward, forcing one foot in front of the other. After all this was what she'd longed for when imprisoned. Here was glory indeed, the sun going down, touching the surrounding clouds with rays of orange and pink, while in the east the heavens were changing from azure to darkest indigo to true black night. Miriam gazed around and was dizzied by the vista, by the great arc of heaven and earth and sea. Her legs tingled and felt as though they would not support her.

When Miriam reached Maximus she crumpled in a heap on deck, not face first thankfully, it was more a general collapse. Maximus bent kindly down, holding to nothing though also harnessed to the lifeline, and took the instruments from round her neck. By degrees Miriam let go her grip on the lifeline, in order to draw out the log book and note the readings. Her heart beat hard as Maximus shouted atmospherical pressure, elevation, and wind direction to her. She noted them down with a hand shaking in time with the hammering of her pulse.

Once the readings were done, Maximus knelt down beside Miriam, so he wouldn't have to shout to be heard over the rush of wind.

"It is all about equilibrium," Maximus said. "How she stays aloft. The pressure of air below the ship, the stunsails keeping her level, the balloons making her rise but no too high. Not into the rarified air itself, where we would be finding it difficult to breathe."

"If only we could discover that in life, the perfect balance of forces." Lord Q's letter intruded upon her mind. Miriam pushed the thought of it away. What was it beside the beauty and terror of the present moment.

"You are a long-headed one, Miriam m'dear," Maximus said, feeling the knot on her head through the material of the cap. "How I hope this great lump may not lessen your wit and penetration. Have you noticed how every generation thinks those that came before...that they were monkeys in our father's day?"

Miriam wanted to laugh, but then she reconsidered. Wasn't that how she viewed her mother and even, at times, Francis? Zahraa Albuyeh Kodio was something of an adventuress and what the unkind might call a bolter, flying from one man to the next as inclination and opportunity suited. Miriam glanced sideways at Maximus; she was not embarking on such a career, she would not merely borrow power from those that had it.

"I know just what you mean," she said.

"I told you I felt my foster father's presence aboard *Queen Charlotte*? As though the right old bastard were just in the coach or the next apartment. You are shocked, I apprehend." Maximus stopped speaking, turning to check the flotation. The clouds were changing from shades of purple to gray, darkness and the first stars appearing. "When I was a saucy midshipman, I told this foster father of mine I wanted to command a crack ship someday. He cuffed me so hard, I—" Miriam interrupted with a gasp. After a pause Maximus went on in a gentler tone. "Polidari was called in, because he was a foreigner and under obligation to my father. My sight was saved, but ever after he behaved different toward me. As though he resented the freakish look of me, the cause of which only he, I, and Polidari know."

"Oh Maximus!" Miriam cried. "I'm sorry, but what a perfect monster of iniquity. You must surely not still feel your looks, that is, your eyes are in any way—"

"No, I don't." He grasped her hand and put it on the lifeline. "Stand up slowly now, Miss Miriam, and we shall walk aft together. I don't feel freakish, not since you have been so good as to see past the outside colour of things."

Miriam's step was livelier, more confident on the exposed deck with Maximus beside her. The Captain stopped to consult with Mr. Dashwood, overseeing the men at the braziers and the voltaic pile. Grasping the lifeline with one hand and a stanchion with the other, Miriam gazed up and around at the enormity of the heavens. The stars shining out ever more numerous in the sky, the clouds close in to the ship and passing right over her, the dimming panorama below of sea and islands and coastline. Vistas like these put heart into her when she was at her lowest ebb. Miriam wanted to be one of *Nonesuch's* people, to live among those who took to the sea and sky.

When Maximus returned to her, Miriam said, "Can you stand to hear more Persian poetry, do you suppose?"

"If you please."

"'Oh this night! This night, it is fit to inspire, Every heart with the passion of love and desire. May these joys never cease to entrance them, O never; What a night! What a night! be it blessed and for ever.'"

Maximus turned away from her for a moment, raising one hand to his eyes. He cleared his throat. "So fitting, so beautiful and true, like you, dear Miriam."

"No, Maximus, like this." Miriam gestured at the heavens through which they sailed.

"Which reminds me of what I was telling you earlier of equilibrium," he said, "and how important it is for the operation of a crack ship. I may have had a hard knock or two coming up, but to be captain of this ship, to sail in her with you, to find that I can possess the regard of such a woman as you, that is compensation more than equal to anything I may have suffered along the way."

Miriam felt an inward glow of belonging, to the ship and to her people, from Maximus down to Thrax secreted somewhere in the hold. She even had kind feelings for Mr. Dodd. If Maximus could pass off being nearly blinded as a mere hard knock, Miriam thought she could likewise forgive and endure.

"You are generous, and I am beautiful," Miriam said with satisfaction. "Whereas our forebears are unimaginative, unromantic, and at once brutish and pretentious. And yet...were not they the ones who dreamed of all this?" She waved her arm, meaning to encompass the ship and her incredible method of sailing. "Are other crack ships out there?"

He shook his head. "No one knows how many there are, except possibly that right old bas..., that is to say, Lord Q."

"Oh him!" Miriam tried to sound unconcerned but that masterpiece of deception, Lord Q's letter, would rise in her consciousness. She would not allow it to spoil her pleasure, the exhilaration of how equilibrium felt, up in the ether. "Do you know how that poem ends?"

"Oh aye. I do read you know." He gave her a coquettish smile, out of keeping with the odd eyes, the sun and wind burned skin, and the flaming red tendrils escaping his cap and whipping in front of his face. "'Though the lamps are all burning, the guests are now gone, and the bride and the bridegroom left happy alone.'"

Miriam was happy, on the deck of a ship thousands of feet in the air. Whatever might come to pass she had experience to sustain her, the good and the bad and the sublime: Like the present one. So high were her spirits that Miriam even allowed into imagination children with the man beside her, in some golden distant future, who would be brought up differently than she and Maximus had been. She would put their abilities and capabilities before whether they might be girls or boys, never dictate what they must aspire to, and so raise no monsters of vanity, iniquity, and entitlement. The notion made Miriam smile, her heart for once truly light and merry.

Author's Note

An author's note is the portion of a book where I am permitted to address you directly, dear reader. I wanted to use this opportunity to note those words in GOLDEN DRAGON that aren't my own, and where not attributed in the novel, provide the sources where I encountered them.

Persian characters in the book are fond of quoting poetry, engaging at times in their own versions of poetry slams, and rightly proud of such national treasures as Hafiz, Sa'di and Rumi. The following two books were the sources for the Persian poetry quoted in GOLDEN DRAGON.

Customs and Manners of the Women of Persia and Their Domestic Superstitions, translated from the Original Persian Manuscript by James Atkinson (ebook available free on line)

The Education of Women and the Vices of Men, Two Qajar Tracts, translated from the Persian and with an introduction by Hasan Javadi and Willem Floor

The letter that opens Chapter Three was written by Edward Pellew, Admiral Lord Exmouth, commander of the combined Anglo-Dutch Fleet that bombarded Algiers on August 27, 1816. The Edward Pellew, Admiral Lord Exmouth of historical fact was a remarkable man. One bearing no resemblance to my fictional character, I'm sure—please see Publisher's Note at the beginning of the book. Everything in GOLDEN DRAGON is made up, except where it isn't.

Finally, although I may take liberties with the historical record and historical personages, I would never wittingly do so with a culture not my own. Many cultures and ethnicities are included in GOLDEN DRAGON, I believe we need more books with diverse characters, but this is a work of historical fantasy. Any errors, omissions, etc., are entirely my own.

Thank you, esteemed and patient reader, for indulging me in this Author's Note. The first one I've had the courage to present.

V.E. Ulett